GODS, TITANS AND MONSTERS

A MYTHOLOGICAL FANTASY OMNIBUS

THE CHRONICLES OF GREEK MYTHOLOGY
BOOK 1

MICHELE AMITRANI

First Edition 2021 (V.2)

Paperback ISBN: 978-1-988770-22-2

Published by Michele Amitrani.

Cover Design by 100 Covers.

GET A FREE BOOK

Subscribe to my free newsletter and get *Greek Myths*! You also get access to early bonuses and goodies only available to my subscribers.

WOMAN OF DESTINY

BOOK I

1
_____

A BLESSING FROM THE GODS

The first thing I remember is the heat of the forge.

I opened my eyes just in time to see the red light of the flame subsiding as the blacksmith god Hephaestus set the chisel on the table, took a step back, and studied me.

"Stand," he ordered, his voice a booming sound that made me shiver.

I stood, naked in the light of the forge's fire. The god's eyes were black and unblinking as he scrutinized me. After a long time, he reached for a cup and handed it to me.

"Drink."

I drank. The liquid was cool and pleasing in my mouth. It quenched my thirst and filled me with strength. The workshop had been hot before the drink. Now I barely noticed the heat of the fire.

Hephaestus' eyes flicked up and down, tracing the length of my body. For a time he probed my shoulders, breasts, arms, and finally my face. His gentle fingers pushed near my temples. I blinked. Suddenly the workshop filled with colors and shapes I did not see before. What had been little more than a gathering of lights and shadows became a room filled with objects rich with textures.

Hephaestus looked thoughtful while he scratched his thick

beard. The smoke that came out of the furnace was as black as his eyes.

"What is the matter?" The voice, not far behind me, was as sharp as winter's wind. I tried to turn to see the speaker but discovered I could not.

Hephaestus snorted. "She is not perfect."

A long stretch of silence; then the voice replied, "She is good enough."

"Good enough will not do." Hephaestus sighed, suddenly looking tired. "She needs to be the best she can be; otherwise, it won't work."

"I've lost count of the times you said that." I heard footsteps moving away from us, becoming so faint I could barely hear their echo. Then they stopped. "This is not a contest, old friend." The voice again. "She is as good as she can be. It's time to move on. Zeus is growing impatient."

A door closed. Silence followed.

Hephaestus grunted as he picked up the chisel. His eyes narrowed as he studied me. The fire behind him grew stronger.

He put his calloused hands over my eyes. "Sleep," he whispered.

I slept.

∼

I WOKE UP AMONG BODIES.

I pushed myself up, the smell of death thick in the air. I was on a hilltop marked by burned trees and piles of ashes. All around me were corpses, so many they were impossible to count.

Far on the horizon, smoke trailed up into countless columns of gray that got lost among the clouds. I coughed, the acrid smell of smoke choking me.

To the west, buildings were swallowed by flames; entire cities were burning on the horizon. A metallic sound at the base of the hill caught my attention: the clash of metal against metal, interspersed with cries of battle.

The wind brought the iron scent of blood, and the very air seemed an extension of war.

I swirled, breathless. I tried to run away from the hill, tears swelling in my eyes and falling to the dead ground heavy with ashes.

The darkness pressed around me. I became dizzy, powerless. I stumbled; a corpse, perhaps? Lifeless eyes stared at me everywhere I looked. I screamed until my voice was broken.

A clap of thunder boomed high in the night sky. Lightning tore apart the dome of the world, and the sky seemed to fracture into a million pieces.

I closed my eyes to the blinding white, knowing the end was near.

MY EYES POPPED OPEN. I was breathing heavily, my heart slamming against my chest. I moved a hand toward my face and realized my cheeks were wet with tears. It took me a moment to recognize the heat of the fire. I was back in Hephaestus' workshop.

"I did not know she could dream."

I blinked the tears away, and the figure who spoke pulled into focus.

He was short, with a narrow frame and small, obsidian-black eyes staring at me. He looked like a child beside the wide-shouldered Hephaestus.

"You don't know many things, Hermes," the blacksmith god said. "You can add this to the list."

The smaller god laughed. "Tell me one more thing I don't know, brother."

Hephaestus scoffed. "I didn't call you for games." He wiped away my tears with a cloth. "You saw what you came to see. Now, go tell the others. It's time for her training."

Hermes ignored him. "Does she really need to dream?"

Hephaestus shrugged. "Father said she should be as close to men as possible. Men dream. I don't see why she should not."

Hermes moved closer, his sharp eyes narrowing until only a hint of pupil remained. He placed a thumb on my forehead, his expression amused. "What did she dream?"

Hephaestus turned his back to Hermes. He grasped an iron rod from a rack and dipped it into a barrel filled with water. The hiss that followed was his only answer.

"You don't know, do you?" Hermes giggled. "How much of Prometheus' work have you stolen to make her possible, brother?"

The blacksmith turned sharply. "She is *my* original work, Atlas-born." His voice had a fizzling edge to it that wiped the smile off Hermes' face. Hephaestus glanced at me. "She is my best work."

Hermes wiped his thumb on his golden vest. "And yet there are things about her you do not know."

"The Storm-Gatherer himself does not know everything."

"That sounds close to blasphemy."

"It is the truth." Hephaestus carried the bucket of water to the other side of the room. For a moment, he was lost from my view.

Hermes turned his attention to me. "Do you also feel pain, little one?" he whispered.

"P-pain?" I echoed, my voice a rasping sound I was not used to. "I ... I don't know the word."

"Well, then." Hermes took my hand in his and stared at me; his eyes were dark pebbles drowning in a sea of white. "Shall we find out?"

He yanked my thumb all the way back so fast I didn't see the movement. It was like a branch snapping. Then came the agony.

I cried out, the pain so sudden I was swallowed by it.

"Aha!" Hermes clasped his hands, delighted. "This answers my question."

Hephaestus emerged from the back of the workshop. "What have you done?"

"Well." Hermes withdrew. "I should really gather the others."

A flicker of light, and he was gone. Only the echo of his laugh lingered between my sobs.

By the time Hephaestus reached me, the pain seemed as though it would become a part of me forever.

He cradled my hand. "Let me see."

I looked at my finger, its angle wrong. "Pain," I said, teeth clenched.

"I know." Hephaestus' eyes avoided mine. "Welcome to the world of gods."

2

THE GOLDEN GATE

He did not talk much. Sometimes, while he was creating a tool or repairing a weapon, he would hum a song, but I never picked up the words. When he realized I was awake, he would stop.

I got used to his brooding silence, to the creasing of his forehead when he was in the middle of work that required all of his skill. His presence was comforting, like a familiar rock you grow accustomed to leaning on.

The day after Hermes broke my finger, the pain was gone. Hephaestus fixed it by molding a mixture of clay, oil, and water around my hand. When he withdrew to assess the repair, the clay disappeared, and with it the damage Hermes had done.

"Thank you," I said, looking at him with grateful eyes. He grunted. That was his standard answer.

He taught me how to stand and walk, how to hold objects and how to balance them on my shoulder if they were too heavy to carry. Sometimes he gave me minor tasks: washing his aprons, polishing weapons and such. He didn't need me to do those things. He was making sure I grew used to moving my body.

It worked. In a matter of days, I could move without effort. It had become second nature to me.

When he was not teaching me, I watched him making tools

and armor. I felt at peace when he created things. I felt like I belonged.

I was polishing a spear when I sensed his presence looming behind me. I turned, smiling at him.

"Come," he said, not looking at me. He grabbed a walking stick that was leaning near the workshop's entrance and pushed the door open. A chill gust of wind filled the room. The fire of the forge subsided, then died. The room grew dark and quiet.

I followed him outside.

I had never been in the open. For a time, I could not even glance at the sky, so bright it was.

"Keep your eyes open," I heard him grumbling. "You will fall if you don't watch where you are going."

"It ... it hurts," I said, shielding my face from the light as I stumbled forward, trying to keep up with Hephaestus.

"You will get used to it."

The air was cool and pleasant against my skin, but somehow I missed the heat of the forge. That fire was the first thing I saw. It gave me reassurance. And now it was gone.

As my eyes got used to the bright outside world, I noticed our surroundings. We were walking along a pathway made of wide, flat stones. Trees bearing golden and red fruit were all around us. As I walked, I could not help but notice Hephaestus' right leg. The god was trailing it beside him, like a dead weight. He had never walked so much, and I had never noticed him limping.

"Father?"

"I am not your father."

I paused. "Maker?"

"Yes. That is more fitting."

"Where are we going?"

"Somewhere I spend as little time as I can."

I pointed to his leg. "Can't you fix that?"

Hephaestus glanced down and grunted. "I could."

"Why don't you?"

"Because this leg makes me who I am. I don't want to be anyone else."

The pathway brought us in front of a building so massive I

could not see the end. It was made of marble so white, it rivaled the clouds. The golden gate that made up the entrance swung open when Hephaestus placed a hand on its smooth surface. We found ourselves inside a wide corridor with beautiful tapestries, dyed deep purple and red, hanging on the walls. Jars of various colors and sizes flanked us as we walked. A sound came from one of them. Had it been a voice? I examined the jar and listened.

"Don't lag."

I turned toward my maker. "I ... I'm sorry." I gave a last glance at the jar and resumed walking.

An identical golden gate was awaiting us at the end of the corridor.

"We are here," he said, more to himself than to me. His jaw was set hard, and his bushy eyebrows drew closer.

"Is there something wrong?" I asked.

"No." A stark answer that made me flinch. He touched the gate. The doors parted and we moved on. We were inside an immense garden. I saw waterfalls and small lakes, flanked by trees and bushes. The sound of chirping birds escaped from the world of green and blue in front of us.

Hephaestus turned and knelt beside me. His eyes were glassy and unfocused. "Stay here." He opened his mouth, as if to add something more. There was a long silence. Then he shook his head and stood. He walked back toward the gate in silence.

I made to follow him.

"Don't!" He raised a hand to ward me off. "Stay."

"Why?" I froze on the spot. Fear seized me. "Why are you leaving me?"

A shadow passed over his face. The blacksmith god turned his back and I could not see his face. "You are useless."

Heat rose from my chest and I felt pain, different than the kind Hermes had produced, but pain nonetheless.

"Useless?" I said.

"Yes," Hephaestus' voice was dry and distant. "And I have no place for useless things."

He closed the massive golden panels behind him, leaving me staring at the perfect surface of the Gate of Olympus.

~

WHEN I TURNED, a goddess stood before me. Pale-skinned and dark-haired, she wore armor made of silver, her breastplate so polished I could see myself reflected upon the metal.

"Welcome to the House of Olympus, child." She smiled at me. Her eyes were the color of melted snow. "My name is Athena."

I glanced back at the gate, expecting Hephaestus to come back and claim me. The gate remained closed.

"You must have questions." Athena waved a hand, and two high-backed chairs appeared. She sat and invited me to do the same. "Let's hear them."

I looked at the empty chair, then at the goddess who was nodding toward it. I looked back one more time before sitting. The chair's metal was stiff and cold against my skin, so different from the simple wooden stool Hephaestus used in his workshop. "Who ... who are you?" I asked.

"Your tutor," Athena said. "One of several who will train you in many arts."

Again my eyes went toward the closed gate. "Hephaestus—"

"His part in your story is over," the goddess said in a definitive tone. "You will never see him again."

"I don't know ..." I trailed off, not really knowing what I wanted to say. "I don't know ... who am I?" I swallowed. "He ... he did not say."

Athena's smile softened. "You are many things, child, but for now, know this: you are a precious jewel made by the fire of Hephaestus and molded out of clay. You have a purpose, but it is not my place to share it with you. Not yet."

I frowned. "Why was I made?"

"Because the world of men needs you, as nature needs bees to pollinate flowers. You are a unique being blessed by the gods. Never forget that."

A unique being blessed by the gods.

I searched for other questions, but I found none. My head felt light and empty. I longed for Hephaestus' presence.

Athena waited a few more moments, then she rose. "I will

teach you household crafts, embroidery and weaving. Other gods will teach you other talents. Come." She offered a hand, and I took it hesitantly. "Father will want to see progress quickly. Patience is not one of his virtues."

3

THE HOUSE OF THE GODS

My memory of the time I spent in Olympus is blurred, for the most part. I remember only a fraction of what happened in the House of the Gods.

Maybe the gods made it so. Perhaps there were things they wished me to forget.

But some things I remember as clearly as lake water.

They each endowed me with one gift, although it's difficult to remember which god gave which gift. There were too many. Only a few remain embedded in my memory.

Queen Hera taught me pride and self-possession. Apollo showed me how to play, dance and sing, while Aphrodite taught me the arts of love. Dionysus instructed me in the arts of self-care, showing me how to dress, care for my hair and for my skin, and how to paint eyes, eyelashes and lips with a variety of colors.

Something else I remember.

The gods gathered in assembly when the time came to decide my name. In the end, they picked a suggestion from Hermes, who had proposed to call me Pandora: *All-Gifted*. A befitting name, they thought, since each of them had conferred upon me a talent.

Always, in the back of my mind, there was the knowledge that one day Zeus himself would call upon me to evaluate the new human he had commissioned from Hephaestus. How could I forget? All my teachers made sure I always remembered.

I dreaded that day, awaited it in agony because I did not know what to expect. If the king of the gods did not like me, would he unmake me? Would he ask the blacksmith god to create a better Pandora? Maybe he would. Maybe he already had.

Those thoughts terrified me. The unknown molded me into a fearful being, always uneasy.

For this reason, I resolved to be the best student I could be. I would learn everything the gods put in front of me, master whatever skill they wanted me to master. I would endeavor to please the immortals. If I was to survive, I needed to be what they wanted me to be.

I don't know how long I spent in Olympus. It could have been a few months or several years. Time flowed in a peculiar way in the House of the Gods. Some days seemed to last too long. Others were gone in a heartbeat.

The Olympians grew fond of me, in the way a master is pleased with a well-behaved dog. They told me I was performing well.

"You are a good learner," Athena said one day, with a proud smile. "Far superior to the male human created by the Titan Prometheus."

Prometheus. A name the gods pronounced with scorn and hate. They called him the Trickster, Lord of Shadows, and Bringer of Fire. He had betrayed them, they said, when I asked what his crime was. He had stolen and gifted the sacred fire of ingenuity to mankind. Because of this crime, the humans gained an unfair advantage over all the creatures of creation, conquering the world. A blasphemy that could not be forgiven or forgotten.

Their hate scared me. These powerful beings did not look noble and bright when they were angry. A dark shadow loomed above them, their eyes like cold stars.

It was one of the rare moments I saw their true nature.

I was too young to judge them, to cast my fragile, ill-formed opinion of the world on them. After all, I was nothing more than a flicker of creation born of their superior powers. Compared to them, I was nothing.

But those moments of dread were rare and far between. To me, the gods smiled and had only words of praise. They tended to me like a gardener tends to his flowers.

But I wasn't a fool.

The Olympians could do what they wanted with me. Hermes had shown me that well enough.

I did not want more pain. I needed to please them, to not draw their attention. Being pleasing was like becoming invisible. It was my best chance of survival.

I LEARNED I was to marry someone living in the world of men, a place the gods called the 'lowlands.' I did not know his name, or why they'd chosen him. The gods did not say.

"Your training in Olympus is almost over," Athena said at the end of a weaving session. "You have learned everything you need to start your new life in the world of humans."

I was scared, but I did not question the gods' decision. I lived to serve.

However, there was something that troubled me.

The night before, I had dreamed again of the hilltop and the burning cities and the countless corpses. Was it an omen of bad things to come?

"You have something you want to say." Athena read my eyes. "Go on. Say it."

I hesitated. I had said nothing about my dark dream. What if they decided I was broken? That my dream was unnatural? That I needed to be replaced?

"Pandora?"

I cast my eyes on the floor, escaping the iron eyes of the goddess. "I ... I dream of death," I said.

"Death?" Athena lifted an eyebrow.

"Yes." I cleared my throat. "When I sleep, I see pain and destruction." I forced myself to speak, even though I felt like hiding underground. "Cities burned by fire, men fighting against each other, choking in blood and smoke, and I ... I see ..." I trailed off; shook my head to clear it of the dreadful images. "I see death everywhere."

Athena walked up to me. She lifted my chin, and I found her gentle smile waiting. "Tell me more about these dreams."

I told her everything. I poured out all my fears, naked in the world.

The goddess listened in silence, nodding occasionally, but she never interrupted.

When I was done, she sighed. "You are the first of your kind, Pandora," she said. "The first woman in creation. There are things even we do not know about you."

"So you don't know what is happening?"

"I think you are having nightmares," she said. "Bad dreams. That's all. Do not vex yourself too much about them. They will go away."

THE LESSONS BECAME FEWER and further between. I was left free to do what I wished, until one day Athena came to my chamber, bringing the news I had waited for my whole life.

"It is time, Pandora," she said. "The All-Father will see you now."

I rose from the asphodel flowers I was tending and followed her in silence.

We walked out of the gates that enclosed the garden and found ourselves in a section of the palace I had never seen.

"Do not fear, child." Athena's voice was bright and lively. "He will be pleased with you. You'll see."

Athena's encouragement did not appease me. To me, those were the soothing words a farmer would whisper to his favorite cow while bringing her to the slaughterhouse.

We arrived in the heart of Olympus, a place the gods called the Sanctuary. I had never been allowed there. The air smelled of incense and burned oak, and the walls were made of a pearl-white metal that glowed with a soft blue light.

This was the place where *he* lived.

"What am I to him?"

Athena's smile had not faded. "You are going to be his gift to mankind."

Mankind. Prometheus' creation.

"You and the other gods spoke often of men," I said, talking because that helped distract me. "But I know little about mankind's story. Who are they, really?"

"They are a promising race," she explained as we walked down an empty hallway. The pungent smell of incense was stronger here. "But they are young and arrogant. A dangerous combination. The fire Prometheus gave them corrupted their hearts. But the gods are fair and just. We seek to bring balance to creation."

We reached the end of the hallway.

"This is where I leave you." Athena pointed to the beginning of a golden stairwell that went so far up, I could not see the end. "Do not fear," she said again. "I will watch over you."

"I am scared."

"Don't be." She kissed my forehead. "You are the best thing to come from Hephaestus' forge. You will make us proud."

4

THE PROMISE OF A JAR

I found the jar at the end of the stairwell. It had been placed at the center of a circular room with walls and floor made of the same gold as the stairs. I walked toward the object and studied it. It was beautiful, amber-brown and as smooth as silk. The lid was sealed with wax.

I looked around. There was nothing else in the room but the jar.

I did not expect to see a god greeting me. The Olympians told me I could not see the All-Father in his true form. His glory would destroy a human's mind in a heartbeat.

But where was he?

"Pandora."

A booming voice seemed to come from everywhere and nowhere. The air was charged with sparkles of blue light and sharp noises, like a crackling thunderstorm in the distance.

I jerked my head. The ceiling became a cloudless sky. I thought I saw a shape in the blue, but the light was so strong I could not keep watching. I diverted my eyes and bowed.

"All-Father," I said, shaking. "I live to serve."

"Hephaestus' work has surpassed all my expectations." The voice came from inside me and outside me. "You are a paragon of goodness. You will serve me well. Stand."

Slowly, I rose.

"Humans." Zeus' voice became my entire world. "They need to be taught their place in the world. Prometheus the trickster betrayed us. He stole the sacred fire and poisoned the humans' mind. You will make them better."

"Me, Sky-Father?" I blinked. "How?"

"The human race is incomplete. The Trickster created the males, but left his work lacking. I will give them what they lack: a woman. The first woman ever made. You are remarkable, Pandora. Through you, I will make them whole and offset the damage done by the Lord of Shadows."

I blinked. "You ... you want to make mankind better?"

"I do." A column of light fell from the ceiling, enveloping me. "Each god has given you a gift. I will give you *two*. My first gift is curiosity, the will to always know more about the world, to seek and find answers to all of your questions."

I heard a sparking in the air and for a moment I felt weightless, a warm feeling infusing my body. Another shower of light hit me, and something suddenly changed in the way I looked at the world around me. Where before there had been uncertainty and fear, now there was wonder and possibilities. I smiled. "Thank you, All-Father."

"My second gift is this jar." A light beam made the object shine. "A token of good luck for you."

"A jar," I echoed. "What's inside?" I asked that question so fast, it took me a moment to realize my lips had moved.

"Ah." I sensed amusement in Zeus' voice. "The first gift is already working. Good. There is nothing inside, Pandora. But promise me you will *never* open this jar, no matter what happens. Swear it. Swear you will never break that seal."

I looked at the jar, feeling strangely empty. There was something about it that made me uncomfortable. But I could not let the king of the gods wait.

"I swear."

"I bless your mission, daughter of promises. May your life bring a long-awaited balance to mankind."

I had other questions for the king of the gods. He had explained little of what he wanted from me, but as I was about to talk, I felt the All-Father leave the room.

"Storm-Gatherer?"

I waited, but nothing happened. Zeus had disappeared.

My eyes were drawn to the jar. I took it and studied it. It didn't weigh much. And yet something seemed odd. For a moment, I thought I heard a whisper coming from inside. I pressed my ear to the surface, waiting. Nothing.

Had I imagined it?

A burst of light appeared a few steps from me, and in my surprise I almost dropped the jar.

A smiling god with winged sandals appeared at my left. "Oh, I'm so sorry," he chortled. "Did I startle you?"

I breathed out, the drumming of my heart loud in the silence of the room. I clenched the hand he injured in Hephaestus' workshop. "You did, Atlas-born," I said.

"Well, nothing better than that to keep you awake." He lent me his arm. "Shall we?" he said with a charming smile.

I hesitated.

"Don't worry," he said with a grin. "No more amusements, I promise. I'm here to bring you to the lowlands, among the humans. Zeus gave the order."

I looked at those dark eyes. They could not be trusted.

But this time Hermes had a mission.

I took the god's arm, and we disappeared from Olympus.

5

UNSPOKEN TRUTHS

The air of the lowlands was heavy with smells I did not recognize. Everything was new and strange. The very sun seemed to cast a different light in the world of men.

Hermes brought me to the outskirts of a forest, thick and lush with green. In the vicinity was a two-story house made of limestone.

"Wait over there." Hermes nodded toward a nearby tree.

I did as he had instructed. I watched him move toward the entrance of the building; then he knocked on the door. A figure emerged from inside the house. He was wide of shoulder and taller than any of the gods. His eyes were huge, the color of a morning sky. I felt my cheeks warm, and I swallowed. Those eyes were the most beautiful things I had ever seen.

"Epimetheus." Hermes bowed low. "I trust you are faring well."

Epimetheus stared at the Olympian. "What do you want, Arcadian-born?" This was said in a sharp tone.

Hermes' smile did not falter. "I come in peace, son of Iapetus. The All-Father recognizes he has been harsh with your brother's creation. He resents that you Titans have been at odds with him for so long. He offers a gift, as a peace offering for—"

"No," Epimetheus cut him off. "Prometheus told me you would come. I will accept no gift from you or any of the Olympians."

The Titan stepped inside and was about to close the door.

"Are you sure you don't want to see the gift first, mighty Titan?" Hermes said. "You've never laid eyes on something like this. And never will. I swear it."

The door remained open; a moment of hesitation. Hermes had piqued Epimetheus' curiosity.

Hermes turned toward me. "Child?" He waved for me to join them. "Come."

I stepped forward, emerging from the shadow of the tree with hesitant steps.

Epimetheus' eyes widened as I moved toward the entrance, my hands clasped around the jar. The Titan's eyes lingered on the flowers Demeter plaited through my hair and on the necklaces of the finest pearls Dionysus had gifted me. I blushed under his stare.

"This is Pandora," Hermes said. "Your gift."

Epimetheus opened his mouth, then closed it.

"May we come in?" The messenger god drew me closer to the Titan.

Epimetheus did not answer. He was too busy looking at me.

"May we?" Hermes repeated.

The Titan blinked; then he stepped aside.

He let us in.

IT WAS love at first sight for both of us.

The gods made sure of it. The way I moved, talked and looked —everything I was—pleased Epimetheus. It was the same for me.

When Hermes returned to Olympus, leaving us alone, we could not stop looking at each other.

It was as though I had known him my whole life. I can't explain it with words. It was a feeling, something buried inside me, like glowing embers covered by a thick mantle of ashes. Once the ashes are removed, the glowing coal can light an entire room.

"I have never felt like this before," he told me, tucking a strand of hair behind my ear. "We were made for each other."

"I feel the same," I said, and I meant it.

The next days passed in a blur of excitement and joy. We were always together.

I learned to read him without effort. He differed from the Olympians, who often said something but meant the opposite. His emotions were open, displayed on his face. He had a kind heart and an easy smile and lived for the moment, enjoying every minute fully, never worrying about the future.

Epimetheus also had powers that made him unique. He could change shape, for instance, and sometimes he did so just to bring a smile to my face. He would turn into a monkey with the legs of a satyr, or into a sheep with the head of a fish. He knew how to make me laugh.

"Is this your true form?" I asked him, glancing at his body.

"It is," he said, blue eyes fixed on me, "but I shrink to a size more befitting to live among men. Otherwise, I would be as tall as this house." He gazed toward his home.

Strength and speed were things he shared with the Olympians, but all of his powers paled when compared with his ability to tell stories. He was a master storyteller. Through his tales, I learned about him and his past. He told me about the Titan War he fought on the side of the Olympians to take the dominion of Cosmos from the hands of treacherous Cronus, and how the world was scorched by the ten-year battle between the new gods and the old ones. He told me about the new order that followed, and of the birth of mankind; how his brother Prometheus molded them out of clay, as Hephaestus had done with me.

I did not have stories of my own. I was young and knew nothing except what the gods had taught me.

"Don't worry," he said, holding my hands and smiling, his eyes two pools of kindness that made me warm inside. "We'll have time to build our own memories. There are good people here, friends who will share stories of their own with us. Let me introduce you to them."

That was my first encounter with men. They lived in a town nearby whose name I could never pronounce. There were hundreds of them, wearing colorful clothes and jewelry. They were friendly and joyful folks who worked the land just enough to get it to bear the fruit they needed. The rest of the time they spent singing, playing and enjoying life.

It took me some time to explain to the townsfolk what I was. At first, they believed me to be some kind of nymph they had never seen. When they understood what I was, they were puzzled but welcomed me all the same. They treated me like a long-lost friend and showed curiosity. They asked me questions, which I answered as best I could.

We went back to the town many times, and each time I learned more about mankind: their daily routine, the tools they used to harvest fruit and hunt, the way they amused themselves in their leisure time. As I spent time with them, Zeus' words were always at the back of my mind, but I did not see the flaw both he and Athena spoke about when referring to Prometheus' creation. Men seemed to be skillful, peaceful people, always ready to share a meal and a good story. I grew to love them.

However, my favorite moments were the times I spent with Epimetheus walking in the forest. We gathered berries and mushrooms and sang songs, birds following us and chirping to the tunes. I loved to discover new things, and the forest was a world inside the world.

"Not that one," Epimetheus said when I picked a plump mushroom with a soft, dark skin and an earthy smell. "It's poisonous. It has killed more nymphs than I care to admit."

I dropped the mushroom and stared at the silver dots that made it look like a night sky.

"It is beautiful, though," I said, wiping my hand on my vest.

"Dangerous things often are."

I turned to regard him. "A bit of poetry, there."

He shrugged. "It's something my brother once said."

"Your brother." I had never seen him. "Where is he now?"

"He is in Crete, I think." Epimetheus did not look at me. "Teaching humans how to cast in bronze."

"You speak little of him."

"There's not much to say. He is a traveler. Always busy. He seldom comes home." He pointed to a patch of ground where a lively red flower grew. "Now look. This flower here is delicious with the barley soup I showed you back at ..."

I listened as he kept talking, but I had not failed to detect the edge in his voice when he spoke of his brother.

Epimetheus was not good at hiding feelings. There was something he did not want to share.

6

BLOOD OMEN

We married the following week. Many village folk came to the ceremony, and nymphs and satyrs sang and played from dawn until dusk.

After we exchanged our promises of love, I smiled at Epimetheus. "You are my husband now."

"And you are my beloved wife." He kissed me. "It's hard to believe the gods brought you into my life. Indeed, you are the best gift I have ever received."

I was happy, and so was he.

I wanted that moment to last forever. It did not.

That night, I dreamed again.

The smoke coming from the burned buildings rose like a shapeless demon clawing toward the sky.

The hill was heavy with corpses. This time, they were arranged one beside the other, in a row. I looked at those faces and discovered with dread that I recognized them. They were Epimetheus' friends. All of them dead.

I stifled a scream as one of those heads turned, lifeless eyes staring at me. "Murderer," it croaked.

"No." I turned and ran away.

Another man blocked the path, his face bloody, a spear piercing his chest. I stepped back. "What ... what do you want from me?"

"Murderer," he hissed. He fell to his knees and gave a final, rasping breath before collapsing on the ground.

I tripped on something and fell on the dusty ground. A hand burst from the earth and seized my leg.

"No!" I tried to free myself. "Let me go!"

Another hand grabbed my shoulder, pinning me down.

"Help!"

"Murderer!" more voices rose from the hill, as a third hand reached for my neck. The ground parted, and I was swallowed into the darkness.

I jerked up, screaming.

"Pandora?" Epimetheus' hand was on my shoulder. "Are you all right, my love?"

"I ... yes," I said, breathless. "It was ... it was just a dream."

"A dream," he said, frowning. "Do you want to tell me about it?"

I thought about the smoke and the blood. I did not want to bring the memory of that horror into his house. "I ... I don't remember," I lied.

Outside, the mantle of night was shrouding the world. The wind offered an interlude of rustling leaves and moving branches. I shivered. Suddenly, I felt watched.

"My love?"

"Yes?" I snapped to attention.

"You are distressed." Epimetheus looked at me with narrowed eyes. "What can I do for you?"

"I ... nothing. I just need—" I cut myself off; looked into his eyes. "Wait. You are very ancient, are you not?"

Epimetheus frowned. "Ancient? Yes, I believe that is a good way to describe me. Why are you asking this?"

"You know many things."

"Many?" He smiled. "I wouldn't say I know *many* things. My brother knows far more than I—"

"He's not here."

"Well, no. He's not."

"You were already old when the Olympians were young. Tell me. What do you know about dreams?"

"Dreams?" He paused, his mouth twitching as if tasting an unfamiliar flavor. "Very little, I am afraid. Dreams are different for gods and humans."

"What do you mean?"

"Titans do not dream, for instance. Only Olympians and lesser gods can. And humans, of course."

I nodded. That was already more than Athena knew.

"Do you know what dreams are?" I asked.

"There isn't only one answer to that question." Epimetheus eyes were far away now. The light of the moon deepened the lines on his forehead. "I once heard the god Moros say dreams are nothing more than feelings settling into memory. If humans are concerned, some gods think dreams are a legacy left from my brother."

I narrowed my eyes. "What does Prometheus have to do with dreams?"

"He has the gift of foresight."

"Foresight? What is it?"

"Sometimes, he can see the future. He told me his gift might have transferred to his creation."

I tilted my head to the side and pursed my lips. "But I'm not his creation."

"No," Epimetheus said. "No, you are not."

I stared outside. I was haunted by the lifeless eyes, the bitter smoke, and sweet-sour scent of blood.

"Pandora, you're shaking. I will fetch a blanket."

"No." I held his arm, pulled him closer. "I am better now. I promise. I just need you to stay with me."

Epimetheus looked at me. He did not seem convinced.

"Please," I said.

"As you wish."

As Epimetheus' arms enveloped me, I closed my eyes and convinced myself I was being silly. Athena was right. My dreams were just dreams. I would not talk about them any longer.

~

WE LIVED A HAPPY MARRIED LIFE. We had our fights, of course, but we always found a way to meet in the middle. Regardless of our differences, our love grew stronger each day. Something else grew that I did not expect: my fascination with men.

The more I spent time with them, the more I was confused about Zeus' spite toward Prometheus' creation. I did not understand why he thought them flawed. They didn't have extraordinary powers, like Olympians or Titans, but they were skillful and ingenious. In their own way, each of them was a small world ripe with possibilities.

Why had he sent me to them? I saw no fault to fix, no damage to repair.

Was I blind?

I could not find answers.

I was sewing in my room, thinking about the reason the All-Father sent me among humans, when Epimetheus asked me a question.

"What is in the jar?" He had been searching for a satchel in which to put dried meat for his hunting expedition. Somehow, he ended up opening the box where I had put Zeus' gift.

I leaped from my chair and put myself between him and the jar.

"Nothing," I blurted. A flush crept across my cheeks. "It's ... it's a gift the gods gave me to remind me of Olympus."

Epimetheus studied it. "It is very pretty. Do you want to display it near the fireplace? It would be better if you—"

"NO!" I cut him off. I grew aware of the drumming of my heart.

My husband's eyes widened. I had never yelled at him like that.

"Forgive me," I said, looking down, unable to meet his eyes. "I ... I prefer it beside me, on the shelf." I took the jar from the box and put it on a shelf over our bed. "There," I said, forcing myself to smile.

"As you wish, my love." He kissed me, picked up his satchel and spear, and walked outside. "I will see you in a few days."

I bid him goodbye at the door.

Outside, a group of townsfolk holding bows and hunting knives were waiting for him. I looked at them disappearing inside the forest with Epimetheus.

When I closed the door, I looked toward the bedroom with a rising sense of dread. That would be the first time I would spend alone in our house.

7

A PROMISE OF DARKNESS

That night, I felt the jar's presence like I never had before. It was as though invisible eyes were watching me. I tried to ignore the odd feeling, calling myself silly for thinking like that.

I was alone. I had never enjoyed being alone, and that feeling about the jar must have been the reason for it.

I tossed in bed again and again, each time growing more impatient. With sleep eluding me and the jar at the center of my thoughts, I had time to think of something I had never considered. Why had Zeus given me a sealed, empty jar and asked me not to open it? Why had he mentioned there was nothing valuable inside? If there was nothing, why take the trouble to seal it? It made no sense.

Or did it? Perhaps there was something of great value inside. A powerful gift from the gods. But Zeus had made me promise not to open it.

My thoughts ventured further. What if, in fact, *that* was a trial. What if Zeus wanted me to *open* the jar?

During my time in Olympus, the gods had always tested me. Every day had been a trial, a new challenge to overcome.

What if this was Zeus' test?

What if I was failing?

No. It could not be. That was just my curiosity.

I had given the All-Father my word I would not open the jar, no matter what. I intended to keep that promise.

THE FOLLOWING MORNING, the feeling changed.

Up to that moment, it had been little more than an afterthought at the edge of my conscience. Now it grew to a pressing feeling that followed me everywhere. It was there when I was cooking, tending to the garden, sewing, washing clothes. I sensed it every moment of the day, no matter what I did to distract myself.

Voices seemed to come from the jar—whispers calling me, luring me closer. It became difficult to concentrate.

In the afternoon, I found myself in the bedroom. I do not remember how I got there, or why. My eyes were tracing the shape of Zeus' gift. There was a fluttery, empty feeling in my stomach. I had been staring at the jar for a long time.

It happened without me noticing it. I caught myself with my hands on the sealed lid, trying to break it. I jerked my hands away and stepped back, gasping. I looked at my fingers, shaking, eyes wide open.

How had that happened?

A whisper came from the jar. I held my breath, clasped my hands behind my back, and got closer to the object. I listened.

Pandora.

I shuffled back a couple of steps, spreading my fingers out in a fan against my chest. A sudden chill hit at my core.

The jar had spoken my name.

I kept listening, afraid of what else it might say. But nothing else happened. The jar remained silent.

Would it remain so? The nameless feeling of wanting to open the jar surged again. The pull was still there—and growing stronger.

It was then that I made a decision.

I would bury Zeus' gift. That would keep this influence from me.

I walked toward the forest, a shovel in my hand and the jar in the other. I dug for what felt like hours, and when I was done, the jar was several hand-spans beneath the ground. I patted the earth flat, exhausted but satisfied.

I turned and went back home, feeling better.

I should have done it long before.

I could forget about the dreaded thing.

IT DID NOT WORK.

The pull to the jar did not subside.

I heard voices. I could not pick up words, but someone was talking. I tried to keep my mind busy with tasks, but the voices were always with me. They made me stop in between chores, followed me when I went to pick berries. They were there even inside the human village.

On my way back home, out of desperation, I went to a lake and jumped in it.

I wanted the cursed chanting to stop. But what I wanted didn't matter. The voices were there, even underwater, plaguing my mind.

Once out of the lake, I cried. I don't know how long I sat on the grass, alone and dripping water, my hands pressed against my ears. "Please," I begged, shaking my head, my throat closing up. "Please stop."

They didn't.

I returned home like a ghost lost inside a nightmare.

I dropped the basket with the berries and fell to the ground, my back against the hard surface of the wall. Time washed over me while I stared at nothing.

Epimetheus came home and found me whispering near the fireplace, my hair a tangled mess, my eyes besieged by shadows.

"My love." He came forward, his voice broken with worry. "Are ... are you well?"

"I am fine," I snapped. I stood and went outside before he could say anything else.

He was concerned, but I did not want him to know what

tormented me. Something wrong was happening, something dark that I could not explain.

What if, after I told him of the voices, Epimetheus decided he didn't want me anymore? What if he discarded me, like Hephaestus had done? What if he stopped loving me?

I could not risk that, so I kept the voices hidden.

I ran away. Epimetheus' shouts followed, like a distant echo fighting for space inside my mind, which was crowded with voices. I kept running. My husband could not see me like this.

I wandered aimlessly in the forest for hours, hoping against hope the voices would stop. The day turned into night, and the temperature fell. The air was crisp and cold against my damp skin. Sweat fell from my forehead.

The light of the moon subsided, and the night grew darker. I looked up. A cloud bank had spread, soaking up the light of bright Selene and the stars.

I found myself in front of the spot where I had hidden the jar. I couldn't remember how I'd gotten there. I turned and ran away.

And then it was in front of me again. I looked around as I ran a hand through my hair. I had run in a full circle.

I fell on my knees, hands holding my head. It was pounding, and it hurt. It felt ready to burst like an overripe pomegranate.

The voices were driving me mad. I could stand them no longer. I needed them to stop.

My hands moved. I was barely aware of my fingers scraping the ground, digging until my fingernails broke and my hands bled. I dug until the smooth surface of the jar was in my hands and I pulled it from its hiding place. Before I could tell myself this was wrong, I reached for the lid. Just a twist, and I would see what was inside. The voices would cease and I would be free to go back to Epimetheus as if nothing had—

An image erupted before my eyes.

A hill, its grass shaved clean by a raging fire. Tall columns of smoke rose everywhere, choking the air. Countless bodies lay broken and forgotten, the screams of the dying a symphony that belonged to the Underworld.

My hand froze on the seal. Tears rolled down my cheeks.

This was wrong.

I was not supposed to open the jar.

I pulled away from it a heartbeat before I broke the seal. I was shaking, my hands cold and numb.

I could not live with this darkness inside. I needed answers, and I knew who had them.

I looked at the sky. "Father of gods!" I drew a breath and released it before talking again. "You asked me not to open this jar, and yet you gave me the one thing that makes me want to know what's inside. Your gift of curiosity is my curse. Why?"

I waited, but no answer came from Olympus.

"Please, All-Father." I swallowed. I needed to ask him the question that had tormented me for days. "Why did you make me to fail?"

The wind on my face was sharp and unforgiving, almost as upsetting as the silence that followed. The cloud bank spread, seeming to soak up the light of the night sky.

Pandora.

A whisper came from the jar. It was soft and alluring. It made me want to say *yes* to anything.

Release us.

The jar was no longer a simple object; it had become bigger, a presence that was pulling me closer and closer to it.

Release us now.

Knowledge swelled within me. Great evil would come from within. I must not open it.

I was weak, sleepless, and tired. How could I resist?

For a moment, the light of the moon broke through the cloud bank. My eyes caught a spark of silver framing the bark of a nearby tree. I blinked; it was one of the poisonous mushrooms Epimetheus had warned me about. I snatched it and brought it to my lips. "I want to know what's in the jar!" I called out, a maddening resolve inside me. "You told me I would bring balance to mankind. I can't do that if I'm dead. Tell me, or I will end myself."

I was depleted, brought to the edge of desperation. I wanted to know the truth.

I was about to speak again when I heard a sharp noise, like a cloth being ripped apart. I turned toward the sound.

She emerged from a slash of light, like a tear in the fabric of the night.

"Child." Athena shook her head, pursing her lips. She looked disappointed. "You are being foolish. Drop it."

I kept the mushroom so close to my face I could smell its sweet, intoxicating scent. "Goddess." I breathed out. "What are you doing here?"

"You are troubled," Athena said, her smile kind and reassuring. "I understand. Let me bring you home. I will make a soothing draught that will make you sleep. You need sleep, child. You will feel restored after. I promise."

Sleep. Yes. I wanted to sleep. But what would happen after?

Everything would start anew.

"You're not here to help me." I cocked my head and raised an eyebrow. "You just want me to open it, don't you? This is what Zeus wants. Why did he lie to me? What's in the jar?"

"Your mind is clouded, child. You are not thinking—"

"I'm not a gift." The words came out in a slur. I swallowed, inhaled sharply, and forced myself to think straight. "That's a lie, too, isn't it? I'm a curse."

"Child—"

"What's inside the jar?"

"I'm disappointed, Pandora. Do you not remember the time you spent in Olympus? We have blessed you with—"

"WHAT'S IN THE JAR?"

Athena's shoulders pushed back and her chest jutted out. She breathed in and said, "Destiny." Her eyes became as sharp as needles. "That's what is in the jar. Mankind's destiny."

Mankind's destiny.

It came to me again. I closed my eyes. The scorched hilltop heavy with corpses. Destruction and death.

A heavy feeling settled inside me. The dream I'd had since the beginning ... It wasn't a dream. It was the future.

"You can't run from it," Athena said as she walked up to me. "The All-Father gifted you with a curiosity so strong it will make you open it, no matter what you try."

I swallowed, the full reality too much to fathom. "I am a weapon. You wanted me to bring destruction."

Athena said nothing. She stared at me, arms crossed, waiting.

I had been a pawn all along, another instrument in the gods' hands. Yes, now I saw it. The gods had made and trained me so that Epimetheus would love me at first sight and would welcome me into his house without a second thought.

And in so doing, doom mankind.

I reached for the seal.

"No." I ground my teeth, struggling against the movement of my hand.

"Don't fight it, child," Athena said, smiling. "It's what we made you for."

Release us, Pandora.

The voices were outside me and inside me.

Do it now.

A sharp smell jerked me awake for a moment. I saw a sparkle of silver embedded in blackness. It was enough.

I inhaled, closed my eyes, and forced my other hand to move toward my mouth.

I bit the soft skin of the mushroom and swallowed it before my hand could twist the cap all the way.

"NO!" Athena's scream made the very air quiver. The jar's voices hissed like cornered snakes.

Shock filled the goddess's gray eyes. A part of me was amused. A novelty: I had never seen surprise on a god's face.

Numbness grew in my muscles and my mind went blank. The world went upside down. I had fallen to the ground.

In the distance, there was a shout and steps approaching. Someone was panting, crying. I was pulled up by strong arms; blue-sky eyes looked at me.

"Pandora." Epimetheus' face was wet with tears. "My wife. What have you done?"

My hand reached for his cheek, and I smiled. "You ... you are the one true gift, husband."

Epimetheus turned toward Athena. "Please, help her! I will do anything."

"The jar," Athena spat, nodding toward the cursed object. "Open it."

I shook my head in horror, tried to pull Epimetheus toward me. "My love. Don't ..."

His firm hands put me down. "Stay here," he said. "I will make this right."

I was too weak to do anything except watch the event unfold.

The seal broke with a snap. A freezing wind rose, bringing the foul smell of rotting corpses. Unholy screams gathered like bursts from a legion of demons coming from Hades. The air filled with a thick, black smoke. Shapes emerged from the darkness. Their sharp eyes, the color of blood, stared at me.

Free. We are free.

The darkness rose and rose until it went west, toward the closest town. Screams rang out as the blackness brought evil and destruction to the men who lived there.

I was exhausted. My eyes closed, knowing my nightmare had become a reality.

The jar was open.

8

A PROMISE OF TOMORROW

I woke up in my bedroom, my head as heavy as a block of marble. But I was alive.

"You almost made me worry."

I blinked. Still drowsy from the sleep, I could not see who was standing on the other side of the room.

"Epimetheus?" I whispered, shaking my head to clear it.

"Not quite."

He moved from the side of the room and came closer so that I could see him. His eyes were as big as my husband's, but instead of blue they were fiery red.

I narrowed my eyes. "P-Prometheus?"

"You were brave, Pandora," the Titan said. "Much more, in fact, than we supposed you would be. Your act of defiance almost destroyed our plan."

I frowned. Something about his voice nagged at me. Had I heard it before? I had. But where? Then I remembered. It was the first voice I had heard in Hephaestus' workshop. He had been talking to the blacksmith god that first day I gained consciousness.

I propped myself up with my elbow and tried to rise, but my head spun. I groaned and lay down again. "What ... what plan?"

"Hephaestus did not believe it would work." Prometheus held something in his hand; a small satchel. "He has always been a skeptical god. He thought Zeus would see through it. But the king of the gods was lacking foresight. His eagerness to punish mankind made him blind."

Punish mankind.

I looked inward and blinked. "Are ... are you talking about the jar?"

"Indeed." Prometheus dropped the contents of the satchel—a pitch-black powder—inside a cup and started stirring with a wooden spoon. "Zeus put in the jar the worst offspring of awful Erebus and Nyx: Death, Violence, Poverty, Misery, Illness and Deceit plague the world. They will forever stay with humankind."

I frowned, surprised at the Titan's careless tone. "You do not seem troubled," I said, doing nothing to hide my confusion. "They are your creation. Aren't you afraid they will die?"

"Will they suffer? Yes." Prometheus stopped stirring. "But die? No, I don't think so. I'm an optimist. Always have been. Here's something else the Storm-Gatherer has never been good at: leveraging consequences. In his eagerness to wipe out mankind, Zeus gave them something far more important than immortality. He gave them *Hope*." He smiled at me. "He gave them *you*."

"Me?"

The Titan handed me the cup, a trail of smoke escaping the rim. "Drink this." He nodded toward the steaming draught. "It will make you feel better."

I shifted my attention to the contents of the cup. It had the same earthy smell of the mushroom that almost killed me. I looked at Prometheus, eyes wide open.

"Yes, this antidote is made of the same thing that almost killed you." He drank a sip, swallowed, then put the cup back on the bedside table. "Most antidotes contain the very poison that can kill. Funny, isn't it? Poison and antidote, black and white, cursed and savior. One thing can be the opposite of itself. It is a lesson we should never forget."

I picked up the cup and sipped.

Prometheus crossed his arms as he watched me drink. "Do not worry. Soon, you will leave this bed and resume your life with my brother."

I swallowed. Already, the warmth of the draught made me feel better. "You said I was *Hope* to mankind." I searched for a reaction on the Titan's face, but I found none. "What do you mean?"

Prometheus looked at his hands, as if the answer to my question was written there. "Zeus was right about one thing: men were flawed. I gave them the ingenuity derived by fire, yes, but it was not enough. They needed something that made them whole." He turned toward me. "You are that something, Pandora."

"I don't understand."

"Mankind had no way to create offspring. You see, the population could grow only if I fashioned more men out of clay. But creating them takes a heavy toll on me, and it has limitations. Thanks to women like you, humankind will propagate in all corners of the world without the help of the gods."

Our eyes met, and he smiled. His eyes were sharper than my husband's, but in them I found the same kindness that made me fall in love with Epimetheus.

"You and your descendants will give your race a sense of family, of history and hierarchy," he continued. "You will pass down your hard-won knowledge to the next generation. Time will make you grow stronger. You will conquer Nature first." He looked outside of the window, up toward the sky. "Then, the stars. Eventually, you will challenge the gods themselves."

I set the cup on the bedside table. I waited for the Titan to say something else, but he seemed content to look out of the window, his gaze lost in the cloudless morning sky.

"What happens now?" I asked.

Prometheus' red eyes went back to me. "Now? We wait."

"Wait for what?"

He walked up to the window and this time looked toward the west, toward Olympus. "Zeus underestimated the one thing that made you different from any other beings who walk the earth; your capacity to rise to a challenge and to adapt. You fall more times than not, and yet you grow stronger each time. Humankind will suffer, yes. But if it goes through the pain, you will prosper and thrive. I don't rejoice in seeing my creation suffer, but it is better than seeing you lost in the trail of history."

"You planned this all along?"

This time, Prometheus' smile did not touch his eyes. "I am not called 'forethought' without a reason."

I looked at him with a sense of foreboding. The Trickster god, the king of Olympus called him. Now I understood why.

I glanced around. I did not hear anyone moving inside the house. "Where is Epimetheus?"

"Gone to fetch some soothing herbs for you." Prometheus turned toward me. "He will be back soon."

"He was afraid you would not allow our wedding."

"I should hope so." This time, he chuckled. "I worked hard to make him believe that. Him and the gods, of course. I needed to make sure they believed I was against your union, when actually I could have asked for nothing better."

"Hephaestus." Remembering him made my chest ache. "He ... he didn't hate me, did he?"

"On the contrary. You are his best work, and he knows it. He treasures you. However, handing you over to the Olympians was a necessity. You needed to be what they wanted you to be. Of course, the good old blacksmith added something more to you than they asked. I'm quite sure not even Zeus knows all the care his son put into his work. It doesn't matter. He will find out."

I still did not understand. "Why did he help you? He is an Olympian."

"He is, but not a blindfolded one. He, too, sees in you infinite possibilities. Hephaestus is a maker, just as humans are. Just as I am. He comes up with new ways of creating things, rather than destroying them. In this, he differs from any of the Olympians. That is why he saw sense in my proposition."

I had so many questions, but my headache was building up. I found it hard to focus. I groaned when the pounding grew to a painful hammering against my temples.

"You need to rest," Prometheus said. "You will need your strength. Your part in the story of humanity has just begun, Pandora." He made to leave the room.

"Wait."

He turned toward me, fiery eyes locked on mine. "Yes?"

"Zeus hates you," I said, remembering the rage I felt when the king of the gods spoke about him. "He will punish you."

"I know." Something in his voice made him sound hesitant. Was it fear? Or something else? He opened the door and turned toward me one last time. "That is *my* destiny."

I SELDOM LOOKED at the sky after the jar was opened. I felt watched, and I didn't want to catch the eyes of the gods. Not because I was scared; just because I had more important things to worry about.

I stopped picking up the berries when I felt the kicking inside my stomach. I laid a hand over my belly and smiled. Prometheus had told us it was a girl. We thought of calling her 'Pyrrha': the color of fire.

The Titan was right: my part in the story of mankind was not over. A new chapter was about to begin.

And it began with war.

Men turned against other men. They spilled blood over the land.

The distance from mankind's biggest settlements spared us from most of the destruction. We heard news of battles breaking in the east and in the west, of cities burned down and built again with high walls and gates; stories of men enslaving other men reached us as well. These things were hard to believe, at first, and yet they soon became our new reality.

The world was changing for the worse. Peace became a brief parenthesis between wars.

Prometheus had been right about that, too.

There was more.

Prometheus told us that a storm was coming. He didn't know when, but he said it would mean death and destruction on a scale never seen before. He suggested that we move as high as possible before it happened, to avoid the worst of it.

"Go to the mountains," he suggested. "You will be safe there."

Eventually, it would become too dangerous to stay near the forest. Its woods and game were precious resources men would seek to build their armies and grow their ranks. Violence and death would reach us, in the end.

But that was the future, and we lived following Epimetheus' calling, not his brother's.

We lived one day at a time.

9

EPILOGUE

I look at my skin and notice wrinkles I don't remember seeing a season ago. Or was it the past year?

Time is a trickster here, in the lowlands. It flows differently from how it does on the tall peaks of Olympus.

Hephaestus' forge is a memory so distant it seems a farfetched fantasy.

I don't even know how many years have passed since the evils were unleashed from the jar.

I don't care to know.

Pyrrha is ten now. Her hair is as red as her uncle's eyes. She is clever, much more than any man I've ever spoken to. This includes most of the gods.

She has a gift. She comes up with ways of doing things faster and better than anyone I know. 'Inventions,' she calls them. A fortnight ago, she made a newly hooked tool to plow the land. Today she invented a sticky substance out of resin that prevents water from leaking out of waterskins and jars.

Prometheus himself is stunned by her abilities and curiosity. I must admit it is amusing to see surprise on the Titan's face.

"She is everything I've ever wanted to see in a human," he said to us, in one of his rare visits. "She is a true promise of things to come."

I could watch my daughter for hours as she moves her hands

relentlessly, creating things that weren't there a few moments before.

She is never still. Her eyes are always looking at something.

Pyrrha also loves to tell tales, to spin stories filled with details and depth. They make me laugh and cry. I sit with her around a fire for hours without noticing the time slipping by and listen to her creating worlds with words. This is something she inherited from her father. I am grateful for that.

When night comes, she looks up at the sky not in reverence, but in *defiance*, like she's trying to figure out a way to steal the stars from the gods.

Who knows? Maybe she will.

One thing is certain. The curiosity Zeus gifted to me passed down to her, and I suspect it will be something every woman will possess. Passed from one generation to the next, it will become part of humankind itself.

I wonder if Prometheus planned this as well.

Smoke rises closer and closer to our home. Cries of war advance to the rhythm of drums and shouts. A decision long postponed is upon us. Epimetheus and I have decided to move deep inland, toward the mountains, just as Prometheus suggested.

I don't know what will happen next.

For now, we are safe. This is all that I care about.

"Mother?"

Pyrrha tugs the edge of my clothes, and I'm pulled out of my reverie. I look down at her. "What is it, light of my soul?"

"I came up with a new way to write stories!"

Her excited expression makes me smile. "Did you, now?"

"Yes! Do you want to see?"

"I can ask for nothing better. Show me."

She takes my hand, pulls me toward the back of the house, then keeps walking.

"Where are we going?" I ask.

"You'll see."

We walk toward the outskirts of the forest. I look around to make sure there are no men around. Pyrrha stops near a fallen tree. I stop abruptly when I realize what's in front of us: the jar.

I stop breathing. "Where ... where did you find it?"

"It was buried over there." She points near the tree. "I was plowing and I hit it."

After that maddening night, I had never asked myself what happened to this jar. I supposed the bursting of all that evil destroyed it. And yet there it is, still in front of me after all this time.

I walk toward Zeus' gift carefully, as if approaching a hornet's nest. I realize I'm shaking. When I am but a step away, I close my eyes. I hear no voices, no dark pull that makes me want to scream. It no longer has power over me.

I breathe out, and open my eyes again.

I find Pyrrha staring at me, her forehead creased with worry.

"Mother? Are you well?"

I look at my daughter with a trembling smile. "Yes, my sun and stars. I am very well."

"Look." She picks up the jar and shows me the inside. "See? I've found a way to write on the inside. The surface is even and easy to mark with signs. If I break it, I will have enough space to write as much as I want." She looks at me expectantly. "Can I ... can I break it?"

I look at the instrument of doom that caused so much suffering; then I put my hands on Pyrrha's shoulders and squeeze them lightly. "Please do."

Pyrrha picks a small hammer from the ground. She swings it at the jar with an excited laugh. The container breaks into a dozen pieces.

I feel like I'm born again.

"Ladies?" Epimetheus' voice comes from the forest. "I'm back!"

"Come." I smile at Pyrrha. "Let us see what your father brought us tonight."

"Yes!" She runs toward her father.

I look at the shattered pieces of what had been my curse, knowing it belongs to a story that no men will ever know.

Or perhaps they will know. One day I might decide to tell the story to my daughter. It's a sad tale, but one from which I learned a lot. Maybe Pyrrha will write it down and pass it along to the next generation.

Who knows who might read it one day.

The end

SOUL OF STONE

BOOK II

1

THE KING AND THE HEALER

I walk toward the golden palace, a much sought-after cure hidden in my travel sack. The colossal gate swings open as I approach, and the first person I see on the other side is the queen herself, there to greet me.

I regard her quickly. She is long past her prime; her hair is more white than black. She wears a heavy line of olive oil and charcoal around her eyes to darken them and beetroot to give a reddish-pink hue to her cheeks and lips.

"Welcome to my house, Panacea, Healer of a Thousand Lands." Her wide smile does nothing to conceal the shadows that besiege her eyes. "We are honored to have you."

"I'm glad you called, my queen," I say, bowing my head. "I hope to be helpful."

"You must be tired, for you have journeyed a great distance." She turns toward a group of slaves waiting by the entrance. "I have instructed them to take care of your needs." She gestures at a tall, handsome, middle-aged man who bows before me. "Pollonio," she says, "bring Panacea to her chamber. Food and fresh clothes are waiting at—"

"Thank you, but I won't need any of that," I interrupt her. "I'm ready. Please take me to him."

The queen frowns. She does not hide her surprise at my boldness. "As you wish," she says dryly. "This way."

We walk into a vast garden graced by a beautiful collection of everlasting chrysalis flowers and rare adamantine lilies. The air smells of damp earth and pine resin.

As we approach the most prominent building inside the property, I note that heavily armored guards stand in front of every entrance.

"What is the king's condition?" I ask as I look at the gold and silver and expensive pottery displayed everywhere.

"He's getting weaker and weaker by the day," the queen says, eyes cast down. "We have tried everything. I've summoned healers from Persia, Egypt, and from north and south of the Indus River. Nothing worked. You are our last hope."

"I understand your pain," I tell her as I smile reassuringly. "Don't worry. I'll do everything in my power to ensure the king lives."

"Thank you, Panacea. I have instructed the workers of the palace to follow your orders as if they were given by myself. You have at your disposal the best physicians, potion makers, herbalists, and healers the city has to offer."

"You're kind, but I won't need them. I've everything I need inside my sack." I shake my travel bag and show it to her.

We walk into the hallway that brings us to the king's chambers. The passage is flanked by countless images depicting the heroic deeds that made him one of the greatest heroes of the civilized world.

At the end of the hallway there is a wooden door guarded by a soldier, and past the door a huge chamber as opulent as the rest of the palace. On the far side of the room, the dying king lies on a colossal bed whose finely crafted frame is of polished cypress. He is half-naked, his skin of a lifeless shade of gray, and his veins are thin and barely visible. My gaze focuses on his bare chest. Three black leeches as long as my hand are fattening with his blood.

A short, white-bearded healer stands as we enter the chamber. Behind him are a dozen slaves, standing motionless and looking miserable.

"My queen," the healer greets her. "I'm afraid there are no developments since the last time you came. I have made sure the king is—"

"Remove those bloodsuckers from my patient at once," I command the healer. He looks at me stunned, as if he hadn't noticed there was another person besides the queen.

"Who is this?" he asks, his eyes lingering on me.

"Tallamo, this is Panacea, the healer I told you about. She has just arrived and asked to see the king. She has my full trust."

"But, your majesty," the healer says, gaping at his ruler. "These bloodsuckers are the only thing that keeps him breathing."

I step forward and face the healer. "According to whom?"

"According to me," Tallamo says, still looking at his queen.

"Then, I'm surprised the king still breathes." I turn and stare at the queen. "I thought I had full license over the king's treatment. Was I mistaken?"

The queen inhales sharply, then looks at Tallamo. "Do as she asks."

The old healer shakes his head but removes the leeches.

I cover the distance that separates me from the bed, assess the king's breathing, then busy myself with the contents of my sack. I take parabellos lotion and mariastera and mix them with seria-root. I produce a runny paste and order the slaves to help me feed the king. They open his mouth and keep it open.

"Swallow this, my king," I say while feeding the remedy to him. His mouth works slowly, then he swallows.

We wait in silence for several minutes, at the end of which the king stirs.

"By the gods!" one slave says. "He's waking up."

The queen puts a hand on her chest. She steps toward her husband. "My love!"

I seize the queen's arm before she can approach the bed. "No," I say. "He needs room to breathe."

The queen stands transfixed. She stares at my hand as if not quite believing it is there.

"Get your hands off her!" the healer warns me. "How dare you touch her?"

"Forgive my forward behavior, my queen," I say hastily, removing my hand and bowing slightly. "It's for his well-being."

The queen regards me carefully. "Then," she says between

clenched teeth, "I shall follow your suggestion." She withdraws from her husband.

"No one could have found a cure so fast," Tallamo says, looking at me without blinking.

"No one who was in this room, apparently," I retort. "Leave me alone with the king. Everyone. There is still much I need to do."

The queen is hesitant, but eventually she nods. "You've heard her. Out."

"You too, your majesty," I say.

"I ..." The queen looks at her husband. "As you wish. Please let us know if you need anything."

The door closes. I sit beside the bed, touch the king's neck, feel the weak pulse. "Can you hear me?" I ask.

The king's eyes flutter. He looks at me, swallows. "W-water," he croaks.

I pour some water in a cup, give it to him.

He drinks and coughs. "Where ... where am I?"

"In your palace, my king."

His eyes wander, taking everything in, then he looks back at me. "Who ..." He swallows hard, wets his lips and starts over again. "Who are you?"

"I'm the only person who knows how to cure you, my king. Your wife called for me, and I answered."

I take a small silver box from my sack. I open it and take out a needle. "This will hurt," I say.

I press the needle into his arm. He winces, then he drags in a shallow breath. "You were right," he says. "It hurt."

Several minutes pass. Five. Ten. The king is unconscious for most of the time. When his eyes reopen, his expression is more relaxed.

"How do you feel now, your majesty?" I ask.

He blinks, then clears his throat. "Like my entire body weighs a thousand sacks of stones. I ... I feel so heavy."

I nod. "It's the effect of the treatment. Tell me, do you remember what happened to you?"

The king looks up at the ceiling. "I was ... poisoned, I think."

"Filomena's blessing," I say, nodding, "bound with Southerner Radish. Not to mention a couple more ingredients I'm sure your healers have never encountered before. The poison went past your food taster as easily as a breeze through a sieve. It was meant only for you."

The king regards me slowly. "Will you give me your name, or will you keep me guessing?"

I smile. "My name is Panacea."

"Panacea." He rolls my name in his mouth for a while. "I know this name."

"Do you?"

"Yes," he says, studying me carefully. "You must be the same Panacea who's fabled to have cured the Titan Garo from Poseidon's bane, who saved the city of Frigira from Hades' plague and drank from the fountain of Doom and lived to tell the tale. I thought you were a legend."

"Sorry to disappoint you, my king. I'm flesh and bones."

"How did you get here?"

"Your wife is a very resourceful woman."

"Panacea." The king repeats my name as if summoning a spell. A small smile plays on his lips. "I always wondered how a mortal became the best healer in the known world."

"Oh," I say, shifting in my chair. "It's a long story."

"They say those are the best."

"Yes." I look into the king's blue eyes. "Indeed, they do."

"Well." The king's smile makes his face look healthier already. "I have the impression you will be around for a while. Why don't you start from the beginning?"

2

A GUEST IN THE DARK
TWENTY-FIVE WINTERS BEFORE

I entered the cave grasping the poisoned arrow between my thumb and index finger.

A dull light entered from a constellation of small cracks on the ceiling at the center of the cavern. Several stalagmites jutted up from the rocky ground on my left, and I heard water flowing on my right.

My eyes were slow to adjust to the darkness. I saw shadows lurking on the ground, darting away from me as I advanced. It took several moments to realize they were snakes.

I blinked, gripped the bow and scanned the area one more time, focusing on the rock formations rising from the floor.

What at first I thought were odd-shaped stalagmites turned out to be statues of warriors. I moved toward them, knowing I had found what I was looking for. Most of the statues were frozen in a defensive stance, as if guarding themselves from a final blow. The warriors held spears and swords and shields, the last tragic moment of fear sculpted into their features.

My heart beat faster. I fixated on the faces of the warriors who had died an unthinkable death. There were dozens, but I was interested in only one.

"Were you looking for something?" a female voice asked.

As I spun to face whoever spoke, something grabbed my legs. I tripped, fell, and felt a sharp pain in my right foot.

"You should watch where you're going. It's easy to fall in the dark."

I grasped at my ankle, clenched my teeth. The pain was blinding. From the corner of my eye I saw a long snake dart away from me, and I knew why I had fallen.

I patted the ground in search of my bow and arrow. When I found my weapon, I aimed it in front of me.

"Show yourself!" I said.

"I'm here," the voice teased.

I shot the arrow into the darkness. I heard a snapping sound, followed by steps coming in my direction.

"How rude." Another cracking sound, and I knew someone had broken my arrow. "Entering my home uninvited, stepping on my friends, and then clumsily trying to kill me with—" The voice paused, amused. "A poisonous arrow?" Her laugh was long and full of mirth. "That's about the dumbest way someone's ever tried to kill me."

She allowed the light coming from one crack on the cave's ceiling to reveal her. She was tall and fierce. Her skin was snow white and her lips as red as cherries. Snakes coiled on her head in place of hair. She smelled of anemones and seaweed. She smelled like the ocean.

I reflexively closed my eyes.

"Don't be afraid," she said. "I will not hurt you, or turn you into a statue, if that's what you're afraid of."

"I'm not afraid of you!"

"Who are you? You don't sound like my typical intruder."

My leg was burning with pain, but I would face my death like a warrior. I tried to stand, but when I put weight on my ankle, I collapsed on the floor. Grimacing, I settled my back on a rock and looked at the snake-haired woman. "I am Panacea, daughter of Aumarion. You slew my brother Estelios, and I swore I would kill you."

"My oh my." The monster sounded amused. "How old are you?"

"I'm thirteen springs old," I answered with defiance.

"Thirteen springs." She shook her head. "This time they sent a child to do the job of an adult. How very honorable."

"I am not a child!" I shouted. "And no one sent me. I'm here of my own will, to avenge my brother's death!"

"Really? You said your brother's name was Estelios." She turned and started moving swiftly between the statues. "Well, I know the name of every fool who has walked into my cave for the promise of glory. They boast their names right before the end. *Estelios*, though. I have no warrior with such a name in my collection."

"Liar!"

"I am many things, Panacea, daughter of Aumarion, but a liar is not one of them."

Again I fought to struggle back to my feet. I groaned and fell back to the ground.

"Are you hurt?"

"Why do you care?"

"Basic hospitality. It's rude to let a guest feel anguish in one's house. Even an uninvited guest. Let me see."

She came closer, and I withdrew. "Stay away from me!" I warned, raising my fists.

Her eyebrows arched. She stepped back into the darkness. "Very well, then. Enjoy the pain."

She walked toward a massive stone less than ten feet away. From the ground she picked up a tool that looked like a small sickle and started scratching moss from the rock. She collected it in a small sack while humming a tune, moving her head to follow the rhythm.

For a long time I watched her; then I spread my arms wide. "What ... what are you doing?"

"What I was doing before you interrupted. I'm harvesting black mosstock."

"I don't understand. Why ... why don't you kill me?"

"Kill you? Why would I want to?"

"Because I hate you?" I said, uncertainty creeping into my voice. "Because I threatened you?"

"You don't hate me." She sighed, cleaned the small scythe with a rag, and kept scratching the wall. "You hate the monster of the story people told you. You don't even know who I am."

"I know who you are. You're Medusa." I spit the name as if it was poisonous. "You are an evil being who kills men for her own pleasure. You are a destroyer of families. You are a cold-blooded murderer, and you deserve to die."

Medusa's arms stopped and she looked at me, her eyes filled with something I wasn't expecting. There was no anger in them, only sadness.

"I might deserve death," she drawled. "But I'm not what you say I am. What about you, Panacea, daughter of Aumarion? You said you want to kill me."

"Yes," I nodded. "Yes, I said that."

She closed the sack, put the scythe on the ground and then looked back into my eyes. "I know a killer when I see one. You're just a child waving her fists at things she doesn't understand. I've nothing to fear from you. That's why you're alive, and that's why you're welcome to stay here as long as you please. Now, it will be cold in a while. Would you like furs to keep you warm? I have plenty."

"I want nothing from you."

"As you wish."

She turned her back and disappeared into the heart of the cave.

3

A PROMISE OF STONE

Medusa was right. The cave grew colder as the day became darker.

I started shaking, but I didn't care. I would rather have frozen to death than accepted Medusa's offer.

Hours passed and the temperature continued dropping. I looked around in search of Medusa, but she was nowhere to be found.

It was at that point that I felt the snakes gathering around me. At first, I thought they wanted to attack me, but then I perceived their bodies warm against my skin. *Warm.* That detail made me think. I never would have imagined that snakes could have bodies so warm, especially in the freezing cold of that cave. Some of them gathered below my legs; they made a bed with their bodies, upon which I could rest.

I heard steps approaching.

"Hey!" I shouted to the darkness. "What are they doing?"

"They are making sure you're comfortable," came the voice of Medusa. "They've spent a reasonable amount of time in the hot spring below the surface of the cave and thought you could use some heat."

"W-why would they do that?"

"There's something in your smell that pleases them. I suspect they like you."

I looked at the snakes coiled below me. I touched a couple of them lightly. They were smooth and dry, not slimy, as I'd thought. I looked back at Medusa. "How do you control them?"

"Control them?" She chuckled. "They seldom listen to me, doing as they please, when they please. Well, I suppose that isn't all true. If I'm polite, they fetch water and they whisper news from the outside world from time to time. They're like well-mannered cats, but noisier and more stubborn."

The snakes below me hissed their collective reply.

Medusa chuckled. "Ah! They do make wonderful jokes."

"You can understand them?"

"Anybody can understand them."

She handed me a bowl with something in it that smelled like my father's garden.

"What is it?" I glanced suspiciously at the bowl.

"Your lunch."

"I told you. I want nothing from you."

She shook her head, placed the bowl beside me. "Then, I guess my lunch will gather dust."

I saw her peeking at my ankle, then just as smoothly she crouched beside me and took off my leather boot.

I withdrew. "What are you doing?"

"I'm assessing the damage."

"I'll be fine. I just need time to recover."

"You have a broken ankle, Panacea, daughter of Aumarion," Medusa said, assessing my leg. "You're not going anywhere. Might as well keep your strength up and eat your lunch while it's edible."

"You said you didn't kill my brother. How do I know that's the truth?"

"You don't. You just have my word." She glanced at the statues. "The truth is sculpted on those faces. Unfortunately, you can't walk and make sure of this by yourself, can you?" Again she studied my ankle. "Now, will you allow me to help you, or would you rather keep guessing?"

I pursed my lips but said nothing.

"I'll take it as a yes to both questions."

Medusa stood and disappeared. She returned with a long stick and a wooden box that contained a small packet the size of my fist. It smelled like damp leaves. "This will hurt," she warned.

I nodded and braced myself for the pain.

She raised my ankle slowly, placed my leg on top of the box, and pressed the packet lightly against my foot.

"This will decrease the swelling," she said.

I winced. It was cold and made my skin itchy.

"And this will help with the pain."

I smelled the contents. "Jasmine root and filomene?"

Medusa's eyes widened. "You have a good sense of smell. Yes, both herbs are in the concoction. There is also a dash of pepperstar and resinmint. You're an herbalist?"

"Not really, but my father ... well, he taught me my way around herbs."

"A wise man."

My stomach grumbled in the cave's silence.

"Eat your lunch, child," Medusa said, still busy tending to my feet. "I'm tired of listening to your stomach."

I studied the contents of the bowl. Mashed beans and olives with goat cheese. Reluctantly, I chose some food to try. It was delicious. Before I knew it, I had finished the entire meal.

I did my best to ignore the pain while Medusa held my broken bone in place with wood splints made of bark, cushioned with linen. Then she applied a wet grass wrap around my ankle.

"What is that?" I asked, pointing at the grass.

"Coralia," Medusa said, "A riverweed that grows inside this cave." Her eyes flashed on the empty bowl. "Would you like more?"

I blushed. "If you have some left."

Medusa filled my bowl again, and I ate it in silence.

"There." Medusa looked at my foot, now tightly held in place by her bandage. "Don't put your weight on it and you'll be fine." She picked up the long stick and gave it to me.

"What is it?" I said.

"I call it a handcane," Medusa said. "It will help you transfer the body's weight from your injured foot to your upper body."

I turned the long stick in my hands. It had a wooden cuff,

shaped like a half-circle, and a hand grip. The ending part had a broad base made of porous stone.

"How do I use it?"

"Insert your arm into this cuff and hold the grip."

"Like this?"

"Just like that."

"I've seen nothing like this."

"I'm not surprised. It's one of my inventions. I made it out of a spear." Medusa looked at one of the nearest stone warriors. "What once was a weapon has been turned into something that does good. There's a poetic justice in that, don't you think? No matter how much you try to turn nature into an object of destruction, you can always turn it back into something honest and worthwhile. Can you stand? Here, let me help you."

She offered her hand, but I waved it away. "I can do it by myself," I said.

Medusa smirked. "Of course you can."

I propped myself up using the handcane. It took me a few steps to find my balance, but eventually I slogged my way toward the statues. I spent the next hour looking into each stone face. Every time I did, my heart skipped a beat and I was flooded with relief when I realized none was my brother.

When I studied the last face, I collapsed on the ground with a heavy sigh. "You spoke the truth," I said. "My brother is not here."

"You sound surprised."

"I don't understand. Where is he, then?"

"Maybe he went into the wrong cave?"

"It's not funny."

"It wasn't meant to be. Look, you can stay there and brood over your brother's fate all you want. As I said, you're my guest. But if you want a sensible answer, ask me a sensible question."

I looked at her levelly. "People swear he died by your hand."

"People say a lot of things about me. They say my evil has no boundaries. They say I can turn a goat's milk sour by looking at it. But as far as evil goes, I have little to spare."

"But you killed these warriors."

"Yes," she said, "I did, and I don't regret it. They came here for the promise of gold and glory. They threatened me, hurt me. And yet, I always gave them the option of leaving. None of them took it. Yes, I petrified them to defend myself, but I know their hearts were cold stone long before they entered my cave."

I looked at Medusa, beautiful in her fearsome features, and I saw the tiredness in her face.

She walked among the statues like an eel swimming among familiar corals. "Behold Aralon, son of Targatio," she said theatrically, resting her long fingers on the warrior's broad shoulders. "Go to Argos, and everybody will tell you he could slay a boar with his bare hands. He was a mercenary; killed people for a living. He did it to fatten his purse and wanted to kill me for the same reason. He told me so." She looked into Aralon's eyes as if peeking into the man's trapped soul. "Twice I asked him to leave," she said, her hand brushing her lower back absentmindedly. "Twice his sword licked my back."

Medusa moved away from Aralon and resumed looking at each warrior. Eventually her hands landed on the jaw of another warrior, taller and broader than the first. "What of Bastar from Tanagra?" she said, looking at him from head to toe. "He was one of the best hunters the world has ever seen. He wanted my skin to add it to his collection. Well, he got a piece." She pointed at a wide gash on her shoulder. "Before I made him part of *mine*."

She went on, telling me the names of every warrior, their stories and the reason they wanted her dead. In the end, she sat down on a rock, her eyes staring at nothing. "Each of them left a scar on my body. I took their lives in return, and that makes me a murderer. They call me the Dark Mistress, Slayer of Men, Soul of Stone. Maybe they are right. Maybe my soul is nothing but a piece of cold rock that deserves to be shattered." She looked up, her eyes searching for mine. "What would you have done, Panacea, daughter of Aumarion?"

I looked at the statues and wondered what was going on inside Medusa's head. The stories I'd heard spoke of a heartless monster that killed heroes for sport, but all I saw at that moment was a woman with deep lines on her face. Yes, there were snakes on her head, and yes, she looked terrible and dangerous, but how much of the story was true? My gaze shifted to the warriors. I wondered who was the hero and who was the monster.

"I'll ask you again." Medusa stood up. "What would you have done?"

I looked away from the statues and said nothing.

"I guess it doesn't matter now," Medusa said, shrugging. "They died, end of story." She looked at her hands in a mute stupor, then shook her head as if dismissing a thought. "I need to rest. And you need rest, too."

I stood. "I need to go. I need to find my brother."

"You're free to go whenever you want." She pointed to the entrance. "However, I encourage you to stay until you recover. Hospitality means something to me, and I'm sure you would move faster once you've healed. Furthermore, I might want to atone for some of that evil you were talking about."

My foot hurt so badly that it forced me to sit back. "Well," I said, setting my jaw, "in that case, thank you."

"You're welcome. Now, before I forget. I've prepared a better bed for you than rocks and snakes." She pointed toward the wall where she had gathered moss. I walked there and found a mat arranged beside the wall. "This is the warmest place in the cave. The hot spring runs close underground. You'll be comfortable here."

I lay down on the mat. Only then did I realize how tired I had been.

"Sleep now, Panacea. I can see the journey that brought you here was long and hard, and you need your strength. Sleep now— a night of sleep without dreams."

I felt the snakes gathering around, and somehow their presence made me feel cozier. My eyelids grew heavy, and I closed them.

I slept a peaceful sleep without dreams, as Medusa had said, until a sudden scream woke me.

4

THE MONSTER INSIDE

I jerked up abruptly as I felt the snakes around me stirring. Somebody was coming toward me from the cave's entrance.

"Please!" I caught the distant echo of somebody pleading. "Please help my daughter!"

"I shall, woman," Medusa's stiff voice came back in reply, "if you get out of my way. Wait outside! I will let you know when I'm done."

"But I'm—"

"Do as I say!"

I rubbed my eyes and squinted into the distant light from the entrance. I followed the figure of Medusa as she passed beside me. The screams I heard intensified.

"What's happening?" I asked, still half asleep.

Medusa didn't reply. I rubbed my eyes again. She was carrying something in her arms. No, not something. Someone. A girl.

Medusa laid the girl on a shiny rock shaped like a low, wide table. The stone had been rounded, smoothed, and polished, and it glinted like wet marble.

The girl had long, brown hair and must have been seven, maybe eight springs old.

"It's all right, child," Medusa said in a reassuring manner, holding her down with both hands. "You're safe." With much effort she started undressing her, then looked in my direction. "Fetch scalding water, salvia and clean linens, you lazy pack of meat!"

For a split second I thought she was talking to me; then I noticed the snakes unraveling below me and darting in all directions.

Slowly, I pulled myself up and used the handcane to walk toward Medusa.

The small girl lay naked and screaming, squirming frantically, trying to evade Medusa's grip.

"This is going to hurt," Medusa said to her, "but I need you to be still." She drew closer until their faces were mere finger-widths away. One of her hair-snakes darted forward and bit into the girl's neck.

"No!" I pushed Medusa away, putting myself between her and the girl. "What are you doing?"

"I'm saving her."

"Saving her? You've poisoned her!"

"The poison is to keep her from moving."

"What?"

"Look at her. She has a splinter as big as my thumb stuck in her stomach. She's too hurt and scared to let me do anything. I need her to be still."

I glanced back. The girl had stopped moving and was silent. She lay flat on her back, as if sleeping.

My eyes widened. "You've petrified her?"

"I could have done that with my eyes, but she wasn't looking, so I had to improvise. Now, move aside, or I will move you."

I moved away, letting Medusa do her job.

The snakes collectively dragged two small boxes and several waterskins to Medusa. They behaved more like ants than reptiles.

"Who is she?" I asked Medusa as I studied the girl. "What happened to her?"

"I don't know, and I don't care," Medusa said, grabbing a water-skin and pouring the contents into a basin. She then took grey powder from one of the small boxes and tossed it on several wooden logs placed under the basin.

The wood took fire in a matter of seconds.

I withdrew, taken aback by the sudden blaze. "Hephaestus himself," I muttered. "How did you—"

"I could use some help," Medusa cut me off. She dipped her hands in the basin and washed them thoroughly. "Can you stand on just one foot?"

"Y-Yes," I said.

"Then I want you to pour water on the wound when I say to." She handed me a waterskin.

I took the container in silence and watched the blood pouring generously out of the girl's wound.

"Hey!" Medusa snapped her fingers. "Look at me."

I looked at Medusa.

"You feel dizzy?"

I shook my head. "No." I swallowed. "I'm fine."

"Good. Come closer and do exactly as I say."

Medusa worked on the wound for a long while and gave me instructions. She had small, sharp tools that helped her take out smaller fragments from inside the wound.

"Pour," she ordered.

I don't recall how long it lasted. To me, it felt like an eternity. At some point there was so much blood that I couldn't see the girl's skin anymore.

As the day grew older and the light became fainter, Medusa handed me a lamp.

"Hold this still. I need more light."

I don't know how she did it, but eventually Medusa managed to stop the bleeding and removed the splinter fragments from the wound.

"Pour all the water you have left," she instructed. After the warm water had washed over the wound, Medusa applied a thick purple paste.

"What's that for?" I asked.

"To prevent an infection," she said.

"What's an infection?"

"Just hold the cursed lamp, girl, and stop asking questions."

I watched her hands move confidently as she finished using the paste and started sewing the hole in the girl's stomach. Finally, she applied riverweed to bandage the wound.

Medusa sighed, her face bright with sweat. "This should keep her from dying." She washed her hands in the basin again and looked at me. "Enjoyed the show?"

"Is she going to be fine?"

"After all I did, she'd better be."

Medusa dried her hands on a linen cloth. "You held yourself together well, considering the circumstances."

I bobbed my head once. "My father was the closest thing to a healer we had in my village," I said.

"Was?" Medusa raised an eyebrow.

"He died two winters ago, taken by a fever."

"What of your mother? Where is she now?"

"My mother? I never met her. She died when I was just a baby."

Medusa nodded. "So you helped your father with the sick and the injured?"

"Yes. I collected herbs for him, cleaned his tools, boiled water, and when he needed, I helped him hold the patients. He also taught me how to create several potions to soothe the pain and to blind the senses. He told me I had a natural talent for potions."

"That's why you're used to seeing blood? Most impressive."

I sat on a nearby rock and looked at Medusa. "How did you do it? I mean, she had lost so much blood. When I realized she had that thing in her belly, I thought she would die."

"No one is dead until they die. There's always something that can be done."

"But you didn't sing," I said, puzzled. "You didn't pray to the gods. You just used those tools and weird lotions and ... and ..." I trailed off, not knowing how to end the sentence.

Medusa scoffed. "Gods." She waved a hand as if dispersing invisible smoke. "Let me tell you something about the gods. They are of no use when useful things are involved. Gods amuse themselves with bets and jokes at the expense of mortals. No, my dear. When you're looking to help the sick and the injured, you want to rely on nature."

"Nature? What do you mean by nature? Nature exists because of the gods."

"Quite the contrary. It exists *despite* them. I didn't need Apollo's favor to fix your broken bone or stop the girl's bleeding. I just needed my skill and the proper amount of ingredients used at the right time. Nature has a drive of her own."

"What is that supposed to mean?"

"It means that the sun will rise and fall tomorrow, regardless of the gods' whims."

"No, it won't! Helios brings the sun across the skies each day from the east to the west in his golden chariot."

"Helios," Medusa scoffed. "I've met that half-dwarf idler once. He was so drunk with nectar he could barely stand on his own feet, let alone ride a chariot from Ethiopia to Hesperides."

"This is blasphemy!"

"Only if you regard the gods with a reverence they don't deserve."

"Well, all right. If the gods didn't help you, someone must have taught you how to heal people."

Medusa fetched a water bucket and started cleaning the polished stone stained with the girl's blood. "In a previous life, my station required me to know potions and herbs, but I was never taught, except that I taught myself. Experience and lots of failures were my teachers. Now, if you're done blabbering, there is a very concerned woman waiting outside the cave. Do you think you could tell her that her daughter is out of danger and that she can have her back tomorrow at dawn? I would go out myself, but I need to make sure she remains stable." She looked at the girl, still sleeping.

"Fine," I said.

I turned and limped away, all the while thinking of what Medusa had said. It was unlikely she could cure people without the blessing of the gods. Every healer I had seen had always invoked them before attending to a patient. However, what really puzzled me was that my understanding of her had been put to the test once again. Not only was she not the monster I thought she was, Medusa was also a powerful healer with no regard for the gods. What else did I not know about her?

It took me a long time to make my way out of the cave without tripping over rocks and stones. Once outside, I was surprised to discover that the sky was streaked with orange and yellow, and the sun was close to the horizon.

I found a woman sitting on the ground, staring at the sea with swollen eyes.

"Hello," I said. "Medusa sends word that your daughter is fine. You don't have to worry anymore."

The woman stood, her hands trembling.

"Is she going to live?"

"Yes. She's going to make it. Medusa will keep her tonight to check on her. You can come tomorrow at dawn to pick her up."

"Blessed be the gods!" the mother said, tears rolling down her cheeks as she looked up at the sky. Then she turned toward me. "Thank you so much!"

I was about to say I didn't do much when she started walking away in haste, probably eager to tell the news to her family.

When I went back inside the cave, I found Medusa brushing the girl's long hair.

"Is she still sleeping?"

Medusa took her hand off the girl's face. "Yes." She cleared her throat. She looked at the cave's entrance. "Is her mother gone?"

"Yes. She's gone."

"Good. I don't need a woman whining outside of my cave and keeping me awake all night."

"Do you often help people like this girl?"

Medusa shrugged. "Some people on Sarpedon know of my skill. Every now and again, villagers desperate enough will bring me their loved ones. I do what I can."

I stared at Medusa's eyes, a thousand questions swarming in my mind.

"What?" she said. "Why are you looking at me like that?"

"Why did you save her?"

"Why?" she snorted. "She was dying, did you not notice?"

"I still don't know why you saved her."

Medusa turned her back to me and started cleaning the tools she had used. "No mother should have to bury her daughter," she said, glancing at the girl. "She's strong; her whole life is ahead of her. I had the power to cure her, so I did."

Medusa dried the tools on a linen cloth, then put them back in a metal box. "Taking a life is easy," she continued, pouring the bloodied water into a crack on the ground. "Preserving life is hard, and that's why it matters. Very few can hold a scalpel and a forceps and keep a life from Hades."

"So you did it to challenge the gods?"

"I did it because it was the right thing to do. As far as this girl goes, who can say if saving her life was a good choice? Maybe one day her son will enter my cave holding a spear. Maybe he'll even succeed where all the other fools failed. Maybe he'll end my curse."

I saw the ground around Medusa's feet teeming with snakes.

"Yes, I know," she said, brushing the snakes' bodies. "I am lucky. I have you, my sneaky little friends."

She walked beside the sleeping girl. "Sometimes, when I'm sleeping, I dream of how it would be to have a child of my own."

"You can't have a child?"

Medusa brushed her belly absentmindedly, then turned.

"You should rest to speed your recovery," she said curtly, turning to walk toward her chamber.

"I've asked you a question."

Medusa stopped. She looked at me over her shoulder. "No," she uttered. "I can't have a child."

"Why not?"

She turned and looked at me with eyes brighter than before. "Because I was denied that gift. You know, girl, you're growing disturbingly interested in me for somebody who just yesterday wanted to kill me."

"You're not who I thought," I admitted. "You said I'm not a warrior."

"I said you're not a *killer*. There is a difference."

"What am I, then?"

"You are little more than a child, Panacea, trying to find your way in the world. I don't pretend to know you, but that is plain enough."

"You're right," I said. "You're not what they said you were, and I'm curious. I want to know more about you."

"So *now* you're trying to make sense of things? Ah, yes. That was to be expected."

"Tell me, were you born like this?" I pointed at the snakes stirring on her head.

"No," she said. "I was born with dreams and promises."

"What happened to them?"

"The gods turned them to stone."

"How?"

"Enough!" she said through clenched teeth. The snakes on her head hissed dangerously. "You're taking advantage of my hospitality, girl. No more questions."

I noticed a red rim glowing around her green eyes. "I just want to understand!" I said.

"Silence!"

Suddenly, I realized I couldn't look away from her. I felt my limbs go numb, and a stabbing pain growing inside my heart. I could no longer move. I felt my fingers and feet go numb. I wanted to scream, but I could do nothing. I kept watching Medusa's eyes glowing with rage.

Agony enveloped my whole being, and I lost any perception of my surroundings. All that was left was darkness and fear; I felt I was on the edge of a precipice, ready to fall.

"Stop it!" Medusa shouted.

I jerked out of that dark limbo. I found myself on my knees, gasping to breathe.

Medusa put a hand over her face and diverted her stare. "Not her!" The snakes on her head recoiled as if a blow had struck them.

A long silence filled with tension hung in the air. Then Medusa said, "I'm sorry," while keeping both hands on her face. "I'm very sorry. I'm tired. I really need to rest."

"No," I managed to say. I stood up, shook my head. "I am the one who must apologize. I shouldn't have asked you those questions. It wasn't my place."

"Everything is forgiven." Medusa glanced at the small girl. "But I have a favor to ask."

"What is it?"

"Will you watch her tonight and wake me up if something seems wrong?"

"I shall."

"If nothing happens when she wakes up tomorrow morning, take her to her mother."

I nodded.

Medusa reached into the baggy fold below her belt. "Tell her mother to give her this herb every day before suppertime for a full moon."

I took the small bag. "I'll remember."

She walked away and then halted. "One more thing. The mother will offer you silver as compensation for her daughter's life. Do not take it. Just ask her to do three good deeds in favor of people she despises. That will repay her due."

I frowned. "Three good deeds? That's it?"

"That's it."

"I'll do it."

For a long time, I stared in silence at the darkness, my heart drumming against my ribcage. I flexed my hands into fists, afraid that the numbing feeling might come back. I now knew what those warriors must have gone through, right before the end. It had been a dreadful state, worse than anything I'd ever before experienced.

It took me a long time to sleep that night, and even when I did, my dreams were plagued by screams and images of people who had turned to stone.

5

A NEW DAWN

The girl woke up as soon as the first reddish light of dawn bathed the cave through the cracks.

I was standing at her side when she started stirring.

"Who are you?" she asked me, confusion in her face.

"My name is Panacea. What's your name?"

"Sophia."

"Rejoice, Sophia." I smiled at her reassuringly. "I'm a friend, and you are safe. Your mother brought you here yesterday. You were injured. Do you remember?"

Sophia looked up, as if trying to summon her last memories. "Yes, I do. Where is she now? My mother?"

"She's outside." I pointed to the cavern's entrance. "How do you feel? Do you have any pain?"

She touched her stomach. "No," she said. "It's just very itchy."

"Can you stand?"

"I think so."

I helped her off the polished rock, fearing she could fall after all the blood she had lost yesterday. It didn't happen.

"Do you think you can walk?"

Sophia nodded.

"Well, then. Your mother is waiting. Shall we?" I led the way.

"I dreamed of a terrible monster," Sophia said as she walked beside me. "She had scary eyes and snakes for hair."

"That wasn't a dream," I said. "It was Medusa, the healer who saved your life."

"That *monster* saved my life?"

"She's not a monster; she's a woman, just like us. Only ... well, I don't know why she looks like that." I thought of what Medusa had said the day before. "I think she was cursed."

"Cursed? By whom?"

I shrugged. "By the gods, I think."

"Then she must have done something terrible."

"I'm not sure about that. Anyway, she's not what people say she is. She's kind and smart and ... well, maybe she's short-tempered and rude and ... what was I saying?"

"Just how kind and rude your friend was."

"I've never said she was my friend."

"It looks like you two are friends."

"Well, I ... listen, she cured me, okay?" I said, pointing to my feet. "And she offered me food and shelter while I'm recovering. I just ... I don't like it when people spread lies."

"Yes," said the girl with a sage nod. "My father always says lies are bad for business. I'll tell all my friends they were wrong about Medusa. How does that sound?"

"It sounds good."

"And could you please thank her for what she did for me?"

"It will be my pleasure," I said as we stepped out of the cave.

Outside, the dawn was fighting off the last remnants of darkness. Sophia trudged forward, and I watched her mother embracing and kissing her as she burst out crying.

"Mom! Stop squeezing me. I'm fine."

"Thank the gods! I thought I'd lost you."

"Your daughter will be all right," I said, reassuring the woman. "Give her this herb every day before suppertime, for a full moon." I handed her the small bag Medusa had given me the night before.

She threw herself at my feet and kissed my boots. "Thanks. I owe you everything."

"I ... I did nothing."

But she wasn't listening. She reached into her pocket and took out a small silver box. "Please take this. It's all I have."

I shook my head. "Keep the silver. If you want to repay your debt, you'll do three good deeds in favor of people you despise."

She looked at me as though I'd made some kind of jest. "I ... I don't understand."

I shrugged. "Neither do I, but that's what she asks."

The mother stood up, dusted her gown and bowed her head. "Then it shall be done."

She thanked me once more, and Sophia waved me goodbye. I watched them slowly walking away, their figures stark black against the gold of the sunrise.

"It's beautiful, isn't it?"

I turned and found Medusa leaning on the cold rock of the cave, looking at the mother and her child.

"What?" I asked.

"The dawn," she said, her eyes still fixed on the two dark specks against the glowing horizon. "It's a fresh start. No matter how much blood was spilled yesterday, it's washed away by the promise of a new day." She glanced at my leg. "Look at you, standing almost straight. You're recovering faster than I expected. You'll be able to walk in no time and go about your business when—"

"I want to be a healer."

Medusa's eyes narrowed. "What?"

"I want to learn how to cure people."

"Why?"

"As you said, taking a life is easy. All you need to do is swing a sword. I see people doing it more often than not. But a miracle like that—" I pointed at the mother and the daughter, "—that's something I've never seen before."

"I thought you wanted to find your brother."

"I will. But first, I want to learn your magic."

Medusa breathed in and out audibly. "It's not magic, it's knowledge."

"Whatever you call it, I want to learn it."

"I'm not a teacher, girl. I have about as much patience as a god has empathy."

"I'm a good observer."

"You're talking nonsense. This is not a fancy you can satisfy in a few days. You need practice and years of toil to be useful. There's a fine line between a talented healer and a butcher. I have no interest in teaching you my craft."

"I'll learn by watching, then."

"Watching? You can start by watching my back turning." Medusa turned and walked into the cave.

"We shall see." I smiled, knowing more than ever that this was what I wanted.

6

THE WEIGHT OF LIFE AND DEATH

The moon filled and died twice after Sophia left the cave.

I used every moment I had to learn from Medusa, even though she was far from thrilled at having me follow her around when she gathered herbs and prepared the ingredients for her remedies, or treated somebody.

People who came to her were usually old or very sick. Many of them Medusa knew by name.

"They are regulars," she said to me one day when I asked her. "They provide me with food and things I need in exchange for my service. It's a trade of a sort. Now stop asking me questions, I'm busy."

Occasionally, we'd get a newcomer, someone like Sophia, people in need of help who had been turned down by other healers.

Medusa accepted them all. When they were cured, she insisted on being paid by good deeds, rather than by silver.

"But why has it to be three good deeds?" I asked her one day after she saved a woman with difficulty breathing. "Why not one, or five, or ten?"

"Because I said so. Now, if you're going to stand there babbling, why don't you pick up that sickle and start harvesting black mosstock?"

Days went by like that. Medusa would not openly teach me

and would occasionally snap when I was in the way. Still, she would allow me to watch.

However, the day I learned the most was when I understood that not even Medusa was infallible.

It was rainy outside when a cart approached the entrance of the cave. A woman came crying out for help, holding a small body covered in blood.

"It's my son!" the mother cried out. "A boar attacked him. Please help him."

The moment I set my eyes on the boy, I felt ill. He must have been the youngest patient I had seen up to that point: three, maybe four springs old. His body was broken, slashed by deep wounds. His face was a mess of dried blood and torn flesh.

Medusa took him from his mother's arms and ordered her to wait outside.

"Prepare the tools and the basin," she ordered me as she laid him delicately on the rock. "I will fetch some water."

The boy never had a chance. He died after three hours. That was the first time I saw a person die on that stone. When Medusa returned the body wrapped in linens to his mother, the woman was silent for a long time.

"Thank you for trying," she said, with no emotion on her face. She looked like a ghost as she laid her son on the cart, pushed it forward, and went away.

Medusa watched her go with her arms crossed. I stood beside her, my arms wrapped around me. Suddenly, I burst out crying.

Medusa glanced at me. "You said you wanted to be a healer."

I nodded, blinked the tears away. "Yes. Yes, I did."

"Do you still want to learn?"

The previous hours came back to me in a flash of images. I saw the boy coughing blood, his eyes white, his pleading nothing more than whimpers. I saw Medusa's face the moment she realized there was nothing else she could do. Then I saw her turning toward me, shaking her head. That was the moment I realized Hades had just won a soul.

"Well?" Medusa pressed me. "Do you?"

"I do."

"Do you have what it takes to spend your nights thinking of something you'd have done differently?"

I searched inside my heart, then nodded. "I do."

"Then nothing I can say will stop you. You will be a healer, and since you're a stubborn little brat, I will make sure you become a great one at that."

"So, you will teach me?"

"Yes. Here's today's lesson: Death is part of the deal. As a healer, you can't take anything personally. Do you understand?"

"Yes."

"Then let's get started."

MEDUSA TAUGHT BY PRACTICE.

In the following days she made me collect herbs, gather mushrooms and dose the quantity of each medicine she asked me to make. Then she made me try my own creations. I wasn't good at the beginning. I had a long stream of stomach aches because of several poorly crafted remedies, and once I almost died of poison. Medusa insisted that this was the best and fastest way to learn.

She was right.

To tell the truth, we didn't see eye to eye on some things. For example, she wanted me to use the water flowing inside the cave stream for our daily chores. She refused to use the fresher water flowing in a river in the nearby forest.

"Why would you want to use this smelly water when you have a better alternative not ten minutes away?" I asked her once when she forbade me to go fetch water outside.

"Because this water is richer in higher elements," she said, "and because you don't know what might lurk in the woods. There are boars, poisonous mantistas, swarms of scorpion hornets and a plethora of things in the forest that are worse. It's also a favorite hiding spot for outlaws, cutthroats, and thugs. It's dangerous, and I forbid it. Do we understand each other?"

"Fine," I said, crossing my arms stiffly. "I won't go."

But I didn't keep my promise.

I sneaked out of the cave more than once while she was

sleeping and got the water I needed to cook and to clean myself. I could be very sneaky when I wanted to.

Regardless of occasional misunderstandings, Medusa was patient in her own peculiar way. She would not let go until I mastered something to perfection. I learned a great deal about potion making and essence crafting. I learned that the right dosage of a poison can save a life. I learned how to mend a broken bone, how to prevent a person from choking to death, how to tame a fever and even how to lengthen life.

When the moon filled up for the third time, Medusa gave me a sharp knife bathed in fire and pointed at our latest patient, a middle-aged man with two arrows in his arm. I had just immobilized him with Medusa's essence.

"That will be your trial," she said. "I will say nothing. Whether he lives or dies is up to you."

I did not fail her. The patient lost much blood, but I saved him. When I knew he was out of danger, I laughed, my hands still stained with blood. I felt like a goddess capable of yielding an incredible power.

"Exhilarating, isn't it?" Medusa said as she looked at me proudly. "That is how it feels to save a life."

7

HEROES AND MYTHS

M ore time passed. Ten, maybe eleven turnings of the sun. I can't remember. I was so focused on my studies, I lost track of time.

One day, while feeding rats to the snakes, I found myself fascinated by the way Medusa spoke with them, and I asked her to teach me.

Understanding them proved to be tricky. It was not so much how the snakes hissed, but how they moved their bodies and for how long that made a difference. Their language had many nuances and could be hard to understand, but eventually that too was something I mastered.

One evening we were right outside the cave, sharing a scant supper after spending most of the afternoon gathering plants. She looked at me over the fire and said, "I don't think there's much more I can teach you, Panacea. What you need now is practice, and you can't get that here, inside this cave." She pointed toward the entrance of her home. "You need to go out there, past the forest, past this island and past the sea that surrounds it."

"But I don't feel ready."

"You will never feel ready, not by staying in my shadow. Panacea, it's time for you to go home."

I looked at her in a mute stupor. I knew she was right, but I was scared. There was so much I still didn't know.

A day later, I went outside early while Medusa was still sleeping, thinking of what she had said to me and dreading the implications. I went to the nearby river to fetch fresh water I'd use for the day. A few snakes had come along to help me carry some much-needed mushrooms.

"White, Sajii," I told a long, fat snake that brought me a big brown mushroom. I waved the mushroom in front of him. "See? This is brown."

The snake cocked his head to the side, hissed briefly and went back to fetch the right mushroom.

I was refilling a waterskin when I heard bushes rustling on the other side of the river. I stood up just in time to see a man emerging from the thicket. He was short and stocky and wearing a long mantle.

"Hoy!" he shouted, looking around. "Is there anybody here?"

I frowned. I was less than thirty feet away from him, with no vegetation between the two of us, and yet he didn't seem to notice me.

I waved my hand at him. "Hoy!" I said. "I'm right here. Can't you see me?"

His head turned toward me but he still did not appear to be seeing me.

"Thank the gods!" he said, collapsing on the ground. "I've been here alone for two days and two nights!"

"What happened?"

"I paid a man to bring me to the gorgon cave, but he tricked me, beat me, and took everything from me. He left me here to die."

I realized his eyes were wandering aimlessly. He stood up, walked forward, and stumbled. "Are you blind?" I asked.

"Yes," he said, standing up slowly. "I lost my sight long ago and heard of the Mistress of Sarpedon, who can cure any illness, so I sold all my possessions and came here to seek her help. But now I have nothing."

"Medusa cares not for gold or silver. She will help you."

"Who are you?"

"My name is Panacea," I said. "I help her as I can."

"Please. Can you bring me to her?"

I walked to the other side of the river. "Come," I said, to guide him. But something hit me hard on the back and I staggered forward. The man, though he was short, caught me before I could fall, then grasped me tightly. I heard the snakes rattling, menacing, but the man drew me closer.

"Send word to the snake-haired bitch!" he bellowed to the reptiles. From the corner of my eye, I saw another man join him. "The Khalos brothers have come to challenge Medusa. Send word to the Soul of Stone that we are here to end her wickedness, with the gods' blessings. Go now, minions of the gorgon. Let her know that if she doesn't show herself by the fading of the sun, the girl dies."

The snakes hissed and then slithered away.

I tried to pull free of my captor. He hit me with the top of his head and I tasted blood in my mouth. Then he squeezed my throat and I blacked out.

When I opened my eyes again, all I could see was blackness. My head was spinning and I could not stop coughing.

"Ah. You're awake, finally."

I moved my head toward the voice. I realized I was inside the cave. I recognized Medusa's figure sprawled over the polished rock.

"Medusa." I shook my head to clear it. "What—" I stopped dead mid-sentence.

Everything came back to me like an avalanche: the fake blind man, his partner, and my foolishness.

"Are you still there?" My mentor's voice was weak and labored.

I stood up and let my eyes adjust to the dim light of the cavern. Then I slowly made my way toward Medusa.

I was shocked at the sight of her. Two arrows were embedded in her side; her dress was torn and soaked in blood.

I remember clearly how staggering it was to see my teacher reduced to that state.

"By the gods," I said, tears welling up in my eyes. "What did they do to you?"

"You should see the other guys," she said, laughing in a breathy, gleeful way before coughing. "They weren't even proper warriors; just small-time thugs looking for a way to get famous. They had no honor, no code. But they were sly. They hit me twice before I subdued them." She spat blood on the ground, then cleaned her mouth with the back of her hand. "I should probably stop talking."

I touched her forehead. She was feverish.

"Are you okay, girl?" she asked me, eyes half-closed. The snakes on her head lay down, silent and lifeless.

Her question, uttered so selflessly, made me angry. "How am I? I have barely a scratch, while you … you … It's my fault. All my fault!"

"Oh, spare me that look. You didn't drag me out of this cave. It was my choice, and I don't regret it."

A dark red pool had gathered underneath the stone. I had never seen so much blood in my life. I swallowed. "I … I will help you."

Medusa snorted. "You're barely standing." She glanced toward the snakes that had assembled around her, looking at their mistress with shiny eyes. "Might as well ask one of my reptilian friends to stitch me up. No, Panacea, we both know I'm well past that point. Now, come closer. There is something I want to tell you before the last sleep takes me and—"

"No!" I cut her off. "I can do this. I can help you."

She looked at me; smiled a thin smile. "I'm fine, Panacea. You really don't have to—"

"Shut up!" I said. "I won't watch you die, Medusa."

Her eyelids flickered open, closed, then open again. Her head rolled to the side, and her limbs collapsed suddenly.

"Medusa!" I grabbed her shoulders. "Please, Medusa! Stay with me!"

"Medusa," she repeated weakly, the shadow of a smile lingering on the corner of her mouth. "That is not my name." Her eyes rolled back and she moved no more.

I checked her breathing: slow but stable. I realized I was shaking. I was scared and angry and utterly lost. But I knew what I had to do.

"I'm going to need your help," I said, turning toward the snakes. They looked at me with their glinting eyes, ready for my command. "Fetch me scalding water and the herbs she keeps in her chamber. I will need them all."

The snakes darted away and summoned more snakes to help them with the task.

I undressed Medusa. My eyes lingered on the scars scattered all over her body. I could see the marks that arrows and swords and spears had impressed into her flesh, year after year. "By the Olympians," I whispered. They were more than I could count.

The snakes came back with what I needed.

I started gathering the tools in front of me and looked at each of them. What would she have done? *Think*, I said to myself. *Think*. "Lay the actions you will make before yourself," I said, summoning back her teachings. "What comes first? What can wait? What is the one thing that will make all the rest redundant?" I closed my eyes, trying to focus not on the unconscious body of my teacher, closer and closer to death, but on the task at hand.

"Stones, pebbles, and then sand," I said. "Deal with the biggest issue first." I wiped my forehead and started moving my hands.

I don't recall what happened afterward. I only remember a sense of focus and control. My hands were moving fast, but not as fast as my thoughts. I had a clear vision of what to do before doing it. Only then did I truly understand how well Medusa had trained me. I depersonalized her. She was no longer my friend; she was a patient needing my help. My emotions were in the way, so I set them in a corner of my heart, chained them with cold assessment, and let my mind do the work.

In time, the snakes, which had followed my every move, grew quiet and still. They were worried; I could feel it. They must never have seen their mistress in that state.

A thousand years after the operation had started, I finished stitching her wounds and prayed to the gods that her body was strong enough to do the rest of the job.

The snakes looked at me, tilting their triangular heads up and down repeatedly. They hissed their collective question with uncertainty.

I shook my head. "I'm not sure," I said. "Her regenerative

powers are better than a human's." I looked at her face, turned pale. "I hope much better."

For two days and two nights, I waited at her side, barely sleeping or eating. The third day, her eyelids fluttered, and I sprinted up.

"Medusa?"

"Oh," she murmured, holding her head up. "It's you again. Must be a nightmare."

I was so happy to see her awake, I burst out laughing. "Who were you expecting to see?"

"Charon, on his stinky boat," she said dryly. "Wouldn't have minded a pleasant view of the underworld across the blackness on the River Styx."

"You will not die, Medusa."

"I suppose I won't." She sat up slowly and looked at her wounds. "Nice stitches," she said with approval.

"Thanks."

"Saved by a girl with barely thirteen winters on her shoulders. I suppose I should give myself some credit as a teacher. I wasn't expecting to wake up."

"I'm humbled by the trust you place in my skills."

She laughed and stopped short. "Ah, that hurt."

"You need to restore your strength." I gave her a cup filled with amber-colored liquid. "Drink this. It'll make you feel better."

She smelled the contents gingerly. "Ah," she breathed out. "Evantal grass and copper root? You stopped my bleeding; now you want to asphyxiate me?"

"It's true," I said, pushing the bowl into her hands. "Healers are the worst patients. Drink."

Medusa made a face, but she drank.

For the next two days, I took care of the cave while my mentor recovered. I checked on her often. She mostly slept, when she wasn't complaining about the food.

On the sixth day, color gathered on her cheeks. She could stand briefly and walk for a few steps, and was very ready to criticize the way I had arranged the rags to dry.

"I'm happy to see you feel better," I said, hands on my hips. "If you can swallow your supper as effectively as you can criticize me, you'll be up and about in no time."

"What is it now?" She sniffed at the bowl I gave her. "Dead rats in onion sauce?"

"It's just carrots, moon mushrooms, and dried meriadok flowers."

"Even worse," she breathed out. She took a spoonful of the meal and winced. "Child, did anybody ever tell you you have peculiar taste when it comes to food? Where is it that you come from?"

"Themiscyra," I said, "near the mouth of the Thermodon."

"Ah!" Medusa tilted her head to the side, staring at me with a knowing look. "Themiscyra! I should have guessed that from the way you move your hips."

I straightened up and looked at her levelly. "How do I move my hips?"

"Clumsily. You Amazons aren't made for walking like women. You're made to run and jump and fight."

"Well, apparently my origin is not really something that shows. I've been told my fighting skills are not exactly great."

"Oh, you are a fighter, Panacea, just not the kind who fights with weapons. Your true strengths lie here." Medusa touched my head, and then my heart. "And here. You are a born healer. That's a gift. Don't squander it."

I looked at her finishing her meal, then I took her bowl away and studied her in silence.

"What are you looking at?" Medusa asked. "I've finished all your cursed meals. Wait. You have more of that?"

"No. I was just thinking of something you said before passing out."

"What did I say?"

"You said your name is not Medusa."

She raised an eyebrow. "Did I, now?"

I nodded. "So, what's your name?"

My mentor looked away, pursed her lips.

"Well?" I pressed her.

She muttered something, probably followed by a curse.

"What was that?" I asked.

"I said, you don't want to know my real name. It sickens me, brings back shadows I worked hard to keep at bay. Ask me no more of my past, Panacea, for it brings me no joy."

"But Medusa, I do want to know your name."

"Why is it so important to you?"

"Because you're important to me, and I want to call you by your real name."

It was like somebody had hit her with a club. She looked at me as if seeing me for the very first time.

"I want to know your story," I said firmly. "I want to know who you really are."

I don't know if it was amusement about what I had said or something entirely different, but she smiled the first genuine smile I'd ever seen on her face. She looked like a girl with not a worry in her life.

"Panacea, daughter of Aumarion, you know how to make your-self heard; I'll give you that. Well then, sit down. This might take some time."

I sat.

Medusa crossed her arms over her chest and started talking, "My story begins in Athens. I was born on a summer day, not far away from the golden beaches of the Aegean Sea. My parents called me Aegana for that reason. My family was wealthy and influential, and they brought me up to serve the goddess Athena, a great honor and a great responsibility. They taught me that serving the spiritual needs of my community must come before anything else. When the eighth spring dawned on me, I became the youngest priestess of Athena's temple." Medusa's hair hissed in chorus, as if they too were sharing a part of the story. Then Medusa resumed talking. "As I grew older, I also grew beautiful. People started coming into the temple more to look at me, at my fair skin, at my long, beautiful hair than to pay homage to the Goddess of Wisdom. It was around that time that I heard rumors that Athena wasn't happy, that she was jealous of my popularity, but I didn't listen. I had given my life to her, proved my allegiance many times over, serving in the temple with dedication and humility."

Medusa's snake-hair grew quiet, as if scared of what was to come. Medusa breathed in sharply and went on. "One day, a visitor to the temple turned out to be much more than that. He was a tall, handsome man with an athletic build and a full, dark beard. He was charming and funny, and he convinced me to walk with him beside the Aegean Sea.

"'You are the most beautiful thing I have set my eyes upon, Aegana,' he said, 'and I want you to be mine.' He flattered me, but I refused. A strong wind started blowing, and the man revealed himself for what he really was: Poseidon, the God of the Sea. He stood before me, and what moments before had been a handsome man became a glorious being. 'Say yes,' he whispered to me, taking my hands into his. 'Don't fear Athena's wrath, for I am Poseidon, the God of Sea and Earthquakes, and I shall shelter you from anything bad. Say yes, Aegana.' I won't deny the truth. I wanted to say yes, but I couldn't. I had sworn to serve Athena by practicing chastity, and I intended to. So I denied him again."

Medusa looked at me, her teeth clenched and her hands balled into fists. "What a fool I was." Then she looked away, staring at the darkness.

"What happened then?" I asked.

She kept looking at nothing, her eyes dull and lost.

"Aegana?"

Hearing her real name, she snapped back to the present. Her eyes came back to mine.

"Have you ever said no to a god?" Her lips trembled. "Not a good strategic choice. The day after I turned down Poseidon, a powerful wind blew open the door of the temple. I was alone when it stormed inside the hallway, threw me on the altar and pushed me down so I could barely move. I closed my eyes, petrified by fear. Then, I felt the wind become something else. I felt hands around my wrists and a body pushing me down. When I opened my eyes again, Poseidon was on top of me.

"'Will you say yes now, Aegana? I'd rather not do this the hard way.' I was so scared, so lost, I didn't know what to do. My lips moved to say yes, but my heart was screaming in defiance. Something inside me said that was wrong, that I should fight. 'Is there something you want to say, my dear?' I felt the iron taste of blood as I bit my lips. 'Get off me!' I spat in Poseidon's face. The god tilted his head back. For a fraction of a moment I felt his grip loosening, his eyes filled with genuine surprise. It didn't last long. Rage filled them. 'Ah, stupid girl,' he said, pressing on me harder. 'This should have been nothing but a fun ride. Now you turned it into a statement. I will enjoy this. You won't.'"

Medusa was breathing raggedly, her chest rising and falling faster and faster. She didn't look at me when she resumed the tale.

"Thrice Poseidon had his way with me. Thrice I yelled for help and no one came. Thrice I died alone in that temple. Poseidon left me there, blood between my legs, my torn dress on the ground. I was twelve years old. Athena found me like that on her altar. 'You,' she said, rage in her eyes. 'What have you done?' To her, I had done something unthinkable. I had desecrated the temple. When I told her I really tried to resist, she stared at me in silence, then said, 'You really tried? How can you say that? You're still breathing, aren't you?' And so she punished me by turning me into this." Medusa pointed at herself.

"I am so sorry," I said to her, tears streaming down my cheeks. "I ..." I trailed off, not knowing what else to say.

I don't know what expression I had on my face, but I saw her smiling at me, as if I was the one needing reassurance.

"Don't be sorry," she said with a soothing voice. "The tale of life is made of such moments. Dark, hurting pieces that shatter our lives." She walked to me, touched my face. "And beautiful moments that make you want to keep going."

That made me cry even more. I hugged her hard.

"Easy, girl," she mumbled. "Your stitches are not *that* good."

We embraced each other for a long time. Medusa gently stroked my hair as I buried my face against her chest, smooth and fresh, allowing myself to process the importance of that moment. Eventually my sobs faded away.

"Feel better?" she asked.

"I should be the one comforting you."

"But you did. You listened to my story."

"I guess so." I pushed myself away from her. I glanced at the water jar and realized it was empty. "I will fetch some water," I said, wiping away my tears, feeling that I needed some time by myself. "From the stream inside the cave," I specified immediately.

"Good," Medusa said. "I can't almost die for you twice."

I made a face, pretending to be offended, then picked up a bucket and headed toward the stream.

I was thinking of Aegana's story and the unfairness of it all. It had never been her fault. I was left wondering about the gods and their pettiness. How could they have done that? Suddenly I heard a noise coming from my left. I turned but saw nothing. I felt watched. I looked around several times. Nothing was moving, and the only sound I heard was the flowing of the cave stream in the distance. I resumed walking.

An invisible hand seized my wrist and pressed it on my lower back. The scream died in my throat as another invisible hand pushed on my mouth.

"Scream and you die," a male voice said. "Where is she? The gorgon?"

The hand lifted just enough to let me talk. "There ... there is nobody here," I shuddered. "Just me."

I felt a blade pressing on my hip. "Lie to me again, and I shall thrust this sword inside you. Now speak the truth. Where is Medu—"

"I'm here."

I could feel the warrior tensing behind me. "Come closer, Medusa," he said. "Do it now, or she dies."

"What are you?" Medusa said. She didn't seem concerned, just genuinely curious. "Reveal yourself. Or shall I call you a coward?"

Silence followed her question. I felt the intruder breathing slowly against my neck, then I saw a helmet tossed on the ground, and suddenly a man appeared out of nothing.

I couldn't see his face, but from the corner of my eye I peeked at the golden shield he was holding. It was so polished it could reflect everything around.

"Ah," Medusa said. "Let me guess. This helmet is Hades' doing, and those sandals smell of pigeon shit. They must be from Hermes. And that shield," Aegana shook her head disappointedly. "That's from Athena, isn't it? What made that bitch decide it was time to complete the job?"

"Speak no more ill words against the gods, monster!" he boomed, waving his sword at her. "My name is Perseus, son of Zeus, and I'm here to end your evil."

"Zeus, you said," she mused. "I don't doubt that. The king of gods has never been good at keeping his cock inside his tunic. I think it runs in the family. What do you want?"

"I want you to come closer."

I could see that the warrior was watching Aegana from behind his polished shield, not looking directly at her.

"You don't need her anymore," Aegana nodded toward me. "Release her."

The warrior pushed me to the side with such strength that I landed over ten feet away. I fell hard on the ground and clenched my teeth in pain. I rolled just in time to see the warrior jumping five feet from the ground and landing on Medusa with his full weight.

The warrior was massive and muscular, his armor as golden as his shield. He must have been seven feet tall.

"I have you!" he said in triumph, pushing Aegana down. He raised the hand holding the sword in the air.

"NO!" I shouted.

Time seemed to slow to a stop. Snakes rained down on Perseus from all directions. They kept him busy but could not get past his sword and shield. He used his body to keep Aegana on the ground, his knees on her back. I could see her wounds bleeding, my stitches gone. Medusa's eyes found mine. She shook her head.

I stood up.

"Stay down!" she ordered.

I didn't. I sprang forward and had almost made it to her when something made me trip. "No!" I felt a snake closing around my legs, then another. "Let me go!" I yelled. More snakes joined the first two. They kept me down and dragged me away from the fight.

I looked at Aegana and dug my fingers into the rocky ground, trying to fight my way back to her. "Tell them to stop!"

In the meantime, Perseus got rid of the last snake that had attacked him, and the cave grew quiet.

"And now, I shall fulfill my destiny." He seized Aegana's hair and pulled her head up. Her white neck looked so exposed and fragile.

"NO!" I cried out. "I beg you! Don't! She's not a monster! She's my friend!"

Perseus looked at me as if I was an inexplicable nuisance, then went back to his sword.

Aegana smiled at me. "It's all right, child," she said. "Remember what I said."

I felt my nails shattering on the rocky ground. "Please," I said, my vision blurred by tears. "Please, let me help you!"

She looked at me and smiled a girl-like smile. "You already did."

The sword dawned on her neck in a flash of silver light. A jerking sound, a tug, and Aegana's head rolled on the ground.

My breath was taken away as I watched this unfold. I stopped fighting and my body slumped down. A part of my mind registered the murderer picking up the head, putting it in a sack and walking away without looking back.

The snakes held me down until the echoes of his steps were a long-forgotten afterthought.

I felt my legs released and I stood. I was shaking so hard my muscles hurt. I walked as though in a dream until I reached the body of Aegana.

The surviving snakes had gathered around her. They poked at her body with their small heads, as if trying to wake her up.

"She's gone," I said, surprised by the stillness in my voice. The snakes looked at me. My hiss had been long and sharp. They glanced at Aegana's body one last time, then withdrew and disappeared into the darkness.

I held Aegana's hand, cold and fragile, and put it on my chest. "I told you I wanted to stay because I wanted to be a healer. I didn't tell you the whole truth." I took her other hand and placed it on my forehead. "See, these past weeks you've been to me the mother I've never known. And now they've taken you away from me." I placed her hands back on her chest and waited a long time before finally standing and walking out of the cave.

Outside, it was cold and dark. The moon was full and round when I gazed up at the sky; the silence was so heavy it felt ominous.

"LOOK AT ME!" I yelled at the starry sky, "Look at me; Poseidon, Hermes, Hades, Athena, and Zeus. All of you cursed gods, look at me! I don't know how long it will take, I don't know how I will do it, but I will make you pay for this. This I swear on her grave."

I stood still, waiting for something to happen. But nothing happened. No one answered my challenge. The gods didn't fall from the sky to make me pay for my arrogance. Nothing moved or stirred, not even a gust of wind. Or maybe that was my answer.

8

GOOD DEEDS

PRESENT

I look into the king's eyes, which have grown still as my story unfolded. "You know something funny, Perseus?" I say, settling back on my chair. "The myth says that the white, winged horse Pegasus sprang from the gorgon's neck. A horse, can you imagine that? It's a lie, but what myth isn't?"

Perseus doesn't move. He's barely breathing now.

I'm aware my hands are shaking. I don't care. My voice is sharp as the edge of a sword when I continue talking. "There's something else the myth of Medusa doesn't say." I put the silver box back into my sack. "It doesn't say that the girl held the body of her friend for hours and cried over a kind soul that history will forever remember as nothing but a monster. But now you know the girl's promise, don't you? Revenge is like a well-aged wine: you must wait to savor it at its best."

The king's eyes are unblinking. "You poisoned my food," he says, dragging out each word.

"Yes," I admit. "I knew no one would have an antidote to a poison I created, and I knew equally well your wife would do anything in her power to save your life. I just had to wait to be welcomed with open arms into your palace."

"Why not let your poison kill me? Why put up this farce?"

"I wanted you to know who did it, and why."

Perseus snorts. "So what's your plan? If you kill me now, you won't get out of this palace alive."

I shake my head. "You forget who you're talking to, Perseus. You forgot what she taught me."

"What is that supposed to mean?"

I nod toward the concoction I'd given him, then I smile. "I killed you before the story even started."

Perseus's pupils dilate as he studies the bowl. When he swallows, I see realization washing over his face. He looks at the door, tries to push himself up with his elbows. "G-guards," he calls out, but his voice is sluggish and hesitant. He touches his neck, where his tendons stand out beneath the white of his skin.

"What do you see when you look at me, Perseus?" I ask him. "They say the eyes are the mirror of one's soul. They are wrong. Eyes are the fine weapons of fear. If you'd looked into her eyes, you would have found dark pits of doom staring back at you. Those eyes were ugly; they could kill, yet she used them to help people when she could. She taught me that to save lives is important. I've learned that lesson well enough. However, I have also learned that there are some lives that are worth taking with no remorse."

"What ..." He coughs, then he looks at me, bewilderment in his eyes. "What ... have you ... done to me?"

"It's curious what happens when you mix her venom with the right dosage of rakish essence," I say conversationally. "You can get the person to stay still while you operate. But add Silvia milk to the mix and something else happens. Your body starts petrifying from the inside out. Legs and back muscles are the first to fade away, followed by arms and throat. It takes a long time to die and you can't move, or talk, you can just feel the pain as every inch of your body slowly freezes to a stop." I lean closer to him and whisper into his ear. "The only difference between you and all the others is that you'll feel the pain for a very long time. Yes, I made sure it happens slowly and painfully. It will take weeks, maybe months. Your wife will try to keep you alive, force food into your mouth, when all you'll want her to do is to let you go. Your mind will be trapped inside a body turned into stone. You'll go insane long before you die. See, Perseus? I'm not as merciful as she was."

I stand up abruptly. Perseus grasps me with his hand, but the effect of the poison has already spread too far. I take his hand off easily. He's struggling to say something.

"What is it?" I ask. "You want to say something?"

Perseus looks at me, the veins on his neck so tight they seem about to explode. "Ghu—" He tries to produce a word, but foam comes out of his mouth. "Agh—"

"Ghu-agh," I muse. "History's greatest hero's last words."

His eyes move wildly and I know his mind is screaming inside a body already unable to move. I revel in his fear for a while, then walk toward the door. I put my hand on the door handle, then stop. I look at Perseus over my shoulder. "I never thought about it," I say, savoring the irony of the moment. "It's funny how sometimes life comes full circle. The beginning is the end, and the end is the beginning. Enjoy your prison."

I go out of the room and close the door behind me. "The king needs to rest," I say to the guards. "No one is to disturb him until tomorrow. Not even the queen. Have I made myself clear?"

The guard bows his head. "It shall be done as you say, healer."

I walk down the hallway. The queen is waiting for me at the end.

"How is he?" she asks, her face tense. "Is he going to make it?"

"He'll live," I say, bowing my head. "But he needs to sleep."

The queen collapses on my feet, crying with gratefulness.

"Thank you! Oh, thank you so much. The gods bless you! What can I give you? Ask me anything, and it shall be yours."

I look at her. "Anything, you said?"

"Anything."

I smile. "In that case, please do three good deeds in favor of people you despise. That will repay your due."

The queen looks at me, puzzled. "Three good deeds? I ... I don't understand."

I smile briefly. "Neither do I."

I walk away from her, away from the hallway and the garden and the palace.

～

THERE IS something I left out of the story. I didn't say how I found out my brother's ship sank long before he reached Sarpedon. I didn't say how I used the past twenty-five years to prepare for my vengeance. I didn't say how I'm planning to make the gods pay for what they did. But Perseus didn't need to know. I will carve this story on the gods' tombstones.

Once outside, in the open air, I can see the city of Mycenae in all its glory.

I look farther, at the sea, and then farther still, at the horizon painted with gold and red. The sunset is vast and beautiful and forgiving. She was right. No matter how much blood was spilled yesterday, it's all going to be washed away by the promise of a new day.

The End

BRINGER OF FIRE

BOOK III

1

THE SEEKER OF SHADOWS

The nomad hadn't lied when he told me about the screams coming from the mountains. After my conversation with him, I would hear his tale many times over from people living in the valley, each of them relating a slightly different version of the same story.

However, the nomad's account, without doubt, had been the most detailed. It was also the only version that offered directions whereby I could reach the peaks and uncover the truth behind the rumors.

Curiosity and my father's love for discovery were two reasons I had decided to undergo the journey, but there was something else that made me persevere, though I didn't want to admit it at the time. The wounds of the past never stop festering. You just learn how to live with them.

I had never been a good climber, and the prospect of traveling in a region with cliffs and sharp rocks did not appeal to me, particularly in those days, when my bad leg failed me often.

For two days and two nights, I rode through the mostly desert region, following the map the nomad had drawn for me. On the third day, a snake with a purple head bit my horse. The poor beast died in a few minutes. From that point, I had to walk.

The next morning, I arrived in a remote village not far from the mountains, a paltry collection of buildings little more than huts.

The inhabitants were dressed poorly, in rags patched together with animal skins. Some appeared to be hunters, as they carried short bows made of dark wood that shone dully in the sunlight. Shepherds, covered in furs, also walked about selling dried meat, milk and hard cheese in the small market at the center of the settlement. A few dark-skinned people sold spiced wine, ale and cider. The village was a mere speck of civilization in the midst of that rocky desert.

I didn't know what to expect when I arrived. The nomad had said that every day at noon the people in the valley heard a noise that sounded like screams booming between gusts of wind. He had said the screams belonged to a shadow demon who had been punished by the gods for some unspeakable crime he had committed. None knew what the crime was, but apparently the screams had been heard since time immemorial. Some said they went back to the beginning of civilization.

Folklore tales can be as colorful as rainbows. If there is something I have learned from my many travels, it is that the more a tale is traded among folk, the more unlikely and fascinating it becomes. And that is why it spreads.

That village was the epicenter of the story. If ever there was a place to find answers, I was in it.

The settlement was so small it had no name—and no place on any map. Most of the people I saw there appeared to be long past their prime. There were more women than men, and none looked happy to be there. Pigs and goats roamed freely among the homes, scavenging scraps of garbage from the dust. The few children I came across ran among the low buildings naked, chasing chickens.

There was a tiny public square in the center of the village, right beside the market. I stopped there and sat on a stone near the village well. It was still early, so I waited for the inexorable rising of the sun.

Noon came, and with it the fabled noise.

It arose from the north, where the mountain peaks rose like gigantic teeth.

In the beginning, I didn't know what to make of the sound. To me it resembled a long, loud wailing from a beast in the process of being butchered. But then, as I kept listening, I heard something else: a prolonged, high-pitched sound. Someone was crying with pain. I could not be sure from that distance, but indeed the noise sounded like screams.

I looked around. None of the people paused or even glanced at the peaks. For them, it must have been as familiar as the dust on the ground. The screams lasted for several minutes, then cut off. The eerie silence that had surrounded the valley hung heavy in the air.

I rose slowly from my spot, and immediately put a hand to my right knee, letting my fingers rub it slowly. I had treated myself poorly in the past few days, eager to get to the village, and now I was paying the price. I clenched my teeth and ambled forward, favoring that leg and doing my best to ignore the pain. I stopped the passersby I came across, one by one, and asked questions.

"What is that noise I heard, good man?" I would ask, offering a smile and pointing toward the peaks. "Kind lady, a moment of your time, if you please. The scream coming from the mountains: What do you make of it?"

For the rest of the afternoon, I asked questions of the people I passed. The answers I got were more or less the same.

"The noise comes from a shadow demon," they would say, "and it lasts as long as the punishment given to him by the gods lasts." As for the punishment itself, no one knew what it was, or why the gods had given it to the demon.

It was exactly as the nomad had said. The people of the village knew the story, but they didn't really have any opinion on the matter. They didn't question the noise, as most men don't wonder about the changing of the seasons, or the movements of the stars. They lived with these phenomena without asking *why*.

Only one of them, a girl who could not have been over ten, asked questions of her own. She had long, dirty-blond hair and huge brown eyes.

"What's your name, stranger?" she asked, after regarding me from behind the stone well.

"My name is Zid," I said.

"Where do you come from, Zid?" She glanced over my wide red cloak and my long wool tunic, hanging over a purple vest. "Your clothes look strange. Your face is odd."

"I come from far away." I pointed toward the valley. "From the west, although the entire world is my home. I'm a traveler, a philosopher and a historian."

The girl frowned at that. I assumed she didn't know what 'philosopher' and 'historian' meant.

"Why did you come?" she asked after pondering my words. Other people stopped to listen to our conversation.

"I came here after learning the story of the shadow demon." I nodded toward the peaks. "I want to unveil the mystery brought by the mountains."

She looked at me as if I had just admitted I wanted to measure the sky. "Then you must be mad," she said, giggling, "for there is no mystery to unveil. You already told me you know the story of the demon, didn't you?"

"I know the story, yes," I said, crossing my arms. "But I will never know what's true until I go out there and find out."

"So *curiosity* brought you here," she said with a bemused smile.

"Well … yes," I said, frowning. "What's wrong with that?"

"Nothing." The girl shrugged. "It just proves you're mad."

I pressed my lips, suddenly aware that people around me were chuckling. "Why?" I asked.

The girl walked up to me. "Why? You're going to go up there, in the wasteland where rocks are as sharp as knives and the wind bites its cold teeth through wool and fur, likely risking your life, just for curiosity's sake?" She narrowed her eyes at me. "What are you, if not a madman?"

I leaned over the stone well and smiled at her. "You have a quick mind and an even quicker tongue, child. You're right. Curiosity is only half of the reason."

The girl wrinkled her nose as she squinted at me. "What's the other half?"

People who had stopped to listen moved on, shaking their heads. Perhaps they, too, thought I was mad. I watched them go and then fixed my attention on the only audience I had left. "It bothers me, not knowing who or what is screaming." The words went out slowly, almost unwillingly.

The girl tilted her head to the side. "Why's that?"

I glanced down, tightly clasping my hands together. For a long time I said nothing, then I looked up, meeting the girl's eyes. "Do you like stories?"

The girl shrugged. "Only the scary ones."

"Do you?"

She nodded.

"Well then." I cleared my throat, feeling a slight heaviness in my chest. "Here's one for you. Many years ago, when I was a boy not much older than you, I lived for a season in a town called Berhun. It was located inside the forest of Argatia, less than a day's ride from the city of Shalayla. Berhun wasn't much of a town, really, but the weather was sunny most of the time, and the air smelled good, a mixture of pines and amber. I liked it a lot." I took a deep breath, my eyes staring at nothing, then resumed the tale. "One day, while I was browsing Berhun's market, I got to like the town even better. A beautiful girl carrying a basket filled with wild berries walked past me. She had long, auburn hair, and her eyes were as blue as lake water. She was the most beautiful girl I'd ever seen. I'd say she was the closest thing to love at first sight I ever experienced. I was a shy boy at the time, but she was so beautiful I decided to summon my courage and go speak to her."

A slight smile played on my lips, and my breath slowed as the memory took over. I noticed the village girl, now sitting in front of me, had fixed her brown eyes on mine.

"I don't remember much of what I said to her that day," I continued, "but she must have thought me funny or endearing, for she laughed and laughed. Her name was Archena, and she lived at a farm a couple of days away from the town. While her mother was selling milk and cheese, we ate all the berries she had found in the forest, and we talked and laughed for hours. When the day grew old and her mother called her, we promised to see each other again on the same day of the following week, when her family would come back to sell more of their products."

I stopped, closed my eyes, and for a moment I could smell the scent of the pines and berries the memory brought back.

"Well?" the girl pressed me when I remained silent. "What happened after?"

I blinked and shook myself out of my reverie. "The next day," I said, "a heavy blanket of fog fell on the whole town. In the middle of the night, I was awakened by a high-pitched sound coming from the forest. I assumed it was just the wind howling, so I closed the shutters and went back to sleep. The next morning I heard many townsfolk complaining about screams coming from a nearby cave. Everyone assumed an evil spirit had taken residence in the forest, brought by the fog, trying to kill people. Hunters stopped searching for game, merchants quit traveling to Shalayla, and woodcutters kept their axes at home, prohibiting their families to leave. The screams continued for two days, then they suddenly stopped."

I wet my lips and a growing heaviness seized my stomach. "A week after, a hunter found the body of Archena, her leg trapped in a depression in the cave. She had survived for days, screaming for someone to help, but her calls for help were all in vain."

"Why are you telling me this story?" The village girl studied me. "You think it was your fault she died?"

"I think it was people's fear of the unknown that killed her."

"And that is why you're here? You think to find a girl screaming for help?"

"I told you, don't know what I'll find," I said. "That's why I'm here."

A long silence followed my statement. In the end, the girl stood up, her narrow face split by a wide grin. "I still think you're a bit mad, but I like you." She sprinted up and glanced at the sky. "It's getting late. I'd better go. Mind your footing when you're out there. The ground is treacherous, even when it looks even. You don't want to break a leg when the wolves come out."

I watched her trot away, her hands cupped around her mouth as she howled like a wolf. I shook my head and smiled. What a weird girl.

I stayed there for a while, breathing in the fresh air, thinking of a boy who knew only how to be afraid. Then, as the temperature fell sharply, I pushed myself off the stone well and started limping my way toward the other side of the village.

≈

I DON'T KNOW exactly how much of my conversation with the girl the other villagers heard, but from that moment on they called me the "shadow seeker." They used that term even though I had offered them my name. To this day, I don't know why.

I spent the next two days restoring my strength and gathering provisions for my journey to the peaks. I traded items from my travel sack—pearls and foreign coins and polished stones—for food and shelter. The villagers seemed to like shiny things the most. The people were friendly but rarely exchanged anything more than a few sentences with me. They kept their distance from someone they believed to be strange, who was wearing odd clothes and asking too many questions. Few of my attempts at striking up a conversation went farther than sharing a few awkward words.

It didn't matter. I would find the truth, with or without their help.

On the last night before my departure, I left the small hut belonging to an elder of the village, who had rented it to me in exchange for a small ceramic cup I had purchased in the western city of Troy. The elder owned a larger hut beside mine.

That night I found him staring at the starry sky, a frown creasing his wrinkled forehead.

"Wise man," I called the elder, "what tales from the sky, this fine night?"

"The sky is quiet," the old man answered, not looking at me. "It has no stories to tell."

I stood beside him and looked at the stars. "When you look up, what do you see?" I asked him.

The elder raised a bushy eyebrow. "I see the eyes of the gods," he said bitterly. "They are not happy."

"Why is that?"

"Because you want to unveil the shadows behind the shadows." He looked at me with a face that bore no expression, then he turned and left me alone.

I shrugged and looked back at the sky. "What do you see, Zid, son of Xhoroast?" I murmured to myself. The answer was simple: I saw bright lights embedded in the night sky. Nothing more than that. I had once met a Phoenician merchant who believed those lights were other worlds where other people looked up and saw just another starry sky. For them, *we* were the small, bright lights. I smiled at that thought. I had liked the idea. Since then, every time I looked up, I didn't feel alone.

I basked in the wonder of creation for a while longer, feeling my muscles relaxing.

Tomorrow I would finally go to the peaks and uncover the mystery. I had spent a long time talking with the villagers and had gathered enough information to get a vague idea of where to head. Unfortunately, since none of these people were interested in looking for the shadow demon, no one was willing to be my guide. That meant waking up at sunrise and setting out alone for the peaks, letting the noise be my guide.

I reached inside my travel sack and took a swig of spiced wine from my canteen. I touched my leg, pushing on the area above my knee, happy that the soreness of the day prior had declined. I would be stiff tomorrow, but I would be walking. That was the only thing I cared about.

From my travel sack, I also took a small object the size of my fist and studied it. It was a small statuette depicting a woman; the last gift my father had given me, and I considered it my protection. I turned toward the peaks, their silent shapes like claws trying to seize the sky.

"Yet another adventure is waiting," I whispered to the night while glancing at the statuette. It was the most precious thing I possessed. It had accompanied me in all my adventures and brought me good luck.

I was relatively young at that time, a few turns of the moon shy of my twenty-ninth birthday. I thought I was ready to face anything.

I was a fool.

Nothing could have prepared me for what I would find in those mountains.

2

THE SHADOW DEMON

I hadn't lied to the village girl. One reason that brought me to the Caucasus Mountains was indeed regret for what had happened to Archena, so many years before. The story of the screaming demon seemed so alike hers I could simply not ignore it.

But there was more.

Even at that time I had traveled enough to uncover the truth behind many mysteries and legends, more than most men would hear in a lifetime. I'd seen many things in my travels. Most were nothing but shadows of fear, a projection of people's discomfort about things they couldn't explain. Screams thought to be heard inside forests, in the deep guts of caves, in the thickness of jungles and in the deepest recesses of the earth scare people because they don't know what produces them. Their ignorance becomes fear, and the fear, often, becomes indifference. And sometimes, indifference kills people.

I had learned that lesson the hard way. I knew the only weapon against indifference was curiosity.

It was with that spirit that I woke up the next morning. The air was crisp, and the wind brought the smell of musk and shortgrass. I left my hut and set out for the mountains.

The temperature had fallen sharply compared with the day before, but by the time the village was a speck in the distance, I had started sweating. Walking wasn't easy, especially with my faulty leg. Dodging stones and fallen trees turned out to be challenging, and the uneven ground offered many perils: exposed roots, treacherous cracks and small debris on which one could easily slip.

I kept walking, hoping my strength would last long enough to reach my destination. I followed the directions given to me by the villagers and kept moving north.

I rested a few times, always checking the sky to make sure of the sun's position. When noon was approaching, I looked around, waiting for the noise to give me the last directions I needed.

I was not disappointed.

Strong and true came the screams, breaking the silence that shrouded the mountains. I headed hastily toward the source of the noise, paying no mind to the growing numbness of my leg.

I had done most of my climbing in the early morning to get here in time, but still I had to climb a few more rocks to get where I wanted to be. I caught my breath and looked up. An odd piece of level ground stuck out of a higher rocky formation. It looked as if somebody had built a platform as wide as a ship's deck on that side of the mountain. The screams seemed to be coming from there.

Carefully, I moved onward, securing my travel sack with a rope around my waist.

Up and up I went, moving toward the platform. While I was climbing, the screams slowly subsided until there was only an eerie silence.

I looked around, waiting for another scream, but none came. I redoubled my efforts.

When I finally put my feet on the platform, I looked at the very spot where the screams had come from.

At first I saw nothing except the wide, flat ground, but then something shiny caught my eyes. Two blue-gray chains, long and thick, caught the sunlight. They were fixed to the side of the mountain, attached to a massive rock a few steps away from me. I stepped forward, and then I froze on the spot.

I blinked when I realized that the rock wasn't a rock at all.

On the hard ground lay *someone*. Not a person; I was sure of that immediately. His head was as big as my torso, his limbs twice as long as a grown man's, thick and bulging with muscles. It took me a few seconds to realize I was staring at a giant. He was naked, except for a torn cloth arranged around his groin. He had no hair on his head. His skin was almost as gray as the rock that surrounded everything.

The giant lay on his stomach, his back curved, his head bowed, his limbs bent and drawn up to the torso. He was motionless, his eyes closed. He looked dead.

The chains were attached to the giant's wrists, binding him to the mountain.

I moved warily, glancing around to make sure I hadn't missed anything else, perhaps another giant in a fetal position. But no; he was the only one. I looked back and regarded the giant with growing uneasiness, a slight chill running down my spine. Only then did I notice the long gash on the upper right portion of his abdomen. There, a stream of a pearl-colored white substance came streaming down his body. I admit the color fooled me for a few moments: it took me some time to realize it was blood.

I was trying to decide what to do when the huge shape grunted. I stepped back reflexively, almost tripping on the stones. My travel sack fell from my shoulder, hitting the ground with a loud thud.

The giant's eyes popped open. They bored into me so intensely I thought they could melt my bones.

Time froze. My senses magnified. I heard the slamming of my heart against my ribcage, the blood rushing inside my body. Faintly, in the distance, I heard the cry of an eagle.

We looked at each other in silence for what seemed like a life-time, the wind sending a shock of icy air that cut through my skin, though I wasn't immediately aware of it. Fear drowned my senses.

The giant looked away from me. He coughed, spitting white blood. His breath came with a rasping sound, like an anchor drag-ging on the bottom of the sea.

I inched back, trying to make no sound as I moved.

The giant coughed again, more blood coming out of his wound. Then he pushed himself to the side. It looked like he was trying to get up.

I didn't stay there to find out. I turned and ran away as fast as I could.

I was halfway to the village before I remembered he was chained. I slowed down and caught my breath.

I looked over my shoulder, expecting to see a huge shape as gray as the mountains following me, but I was alone. I gritted my teeth, ignored the throbbing of my leg, and kept walking.

When I arrived at the village, the people stopped what they were doing and looked at me with eyes full of wonder. I trudged toward the central square, wheezing.

"I saw him," I said with a rasping voice to each person I came across, waving toward the peaks. I must have been as pale as a dead man, because they seemed scared of me. "I saw him on the mountain!"

They alerted the village's elder. The glaze-eyed man who had lent me his hut came out from a low, round building. He nodded when he looked at me, as if he knew a great secret.

"Seeker," he said, his eyes lingering on mine. "So you saw the shadow demon."

I shook my head vigorously, still trying to make sense of what I saw. "No," I breathed out, and then I looked over my shoulder, as I had done countless times during my run. "It was not a shadow that I saw. He was ... he was big and made of flesh." I tried to catch my breath, still thinking of the huge being chained to the rock. His pearl white blood flashed every time I closed my eyes, like the afterimage of the sun.

"He?" a woman said, while holding an infant. "If not a shadow, what is *he*?"

I tried to summon the details, but it was difficult to pin them down. After all, everything had happened in a few heartbeats.

"It was a giant," I said, trying to hold the image in my mind. "As big as three men grown ... and ... and ..." I trailed off, unsure of how to continue. What else? I could not remember.

"A giant," the elder repeated, eyes unblinking. "What kind of giant?"

"I'm not sure," I said, my voice unsteady. Someone offered me water. I drank eagerly, and when my thirst had been sated, I looked back at the elder. "It was a giant, bound to the side of a mountain by a set of long, heavy chains. He ... he looked dead. He was wounded. There was blood all over the place, only ... well, his blood was different. It was as white as snow."

The villagers looked at each other. Some of them murmured while throwing doubtful glances at me, but none of their whispers reached my ears.

"What happened after?" the elder asked.

"He ... the giant looked at me," I said, remembering the intensity of that stare. "He was trying to stand when I left, but I'm not sure he still lives."

"He lives," the elder said matter-of-factly. "For tomorrow, we'll hear his screams as we always have, and as our fathers did, and the fathers of their fathers."

The people nodded, as if the elder had stated an inescapable truth. The old man looked at me, his arms wide open. "Well, seeker. Your curiosity has been satisfied." He smiled, as if a great burden had been lifted from his shoulders. "You found what you were looking for. Will you be on your way tomorrow?"

I looked at the old man incredulously. "I just told you a giant lives in the mountains. He's less than four hours away from your homes. Aren't you afraid he might break his chains and come for you?"

"He won't come," the elder said. "He's chained, and he's not meant to leave."

"You can't know that for sure."

"The gods put him there, seeker," the elder repeated. "That is all we need to know."

"So you won't do anything?"

"What would you have us do?"

"Well, if he's still alive, as you believe, go talk to him. Find out why he's there. That would be a start."

"Why would we do that?"

I looked at them, all of them, one by one. "Is there anybody who wants to come with me to question the giant? Anybody?"

None of the villagers answered. They waved their hands dismissively and went back to what they were doing.

"Seeker," the elder approached me, hands folded behind his

back. "You didn't answer my question. Will you be on your way tomorrow?"

"No," I said stiffly. "No, I won't."

"Will you go back to the demon?"

"I told you. He's not a demon."

"So you say." The elder drew a deep breath. "Once again, you didn't answer my question."

"I don't know," I said, running a hand through my hair. "I will stay for now."

The old man let out a heavy sigh. He suddenly looked weary. "That means you will still need your accommodation. Very well, then, I shall instruct my wife to have it prepared for the night."

When the elder left, all the rest of the people dispersed. I collapsed on the ground, rubbing at my temples, still trying to make sense of what I had seen.

"You look dog-tired."

I started, looked up. In front of me was the girl with ragged clothes who'd spoken with me a few days before.

"Ah," I said with a tentative smile. "You again. Do you still think I'm mad?"

"Did he look sad?" she asked, ignoring my question.

I blinked. "I'm sorry?"

"The giant." The girl played absently with a strand of her dirty hair. "Did he look sad?"

I scratched my cheek. "Um ... sad? I ... I don't know. What kind of question is that?"

"It's just a question."

"Well, your question makes no sense. You know what? You are right. I'm tired." I lifted myself up, painfully aware of my leg. "I'm going to rest."

"Did you lose it?"

I looked at her blankly. "What?"

"Your sack," she said. "This morning I saw you bringing it with you. Now you don't have it."

My hand reached for my back, but grasped nothing but air. I spun and looked around. Nothing. The girl was right. My travel sack was nowhere to be found.

"No," I whispered, a sour taste in my mouth. I traced my path all the way back until I reached the village's outskirts, my darting gaze inspecting the mountains. Could I have dropped the sack while I was—

I bit my lip, a thick feeling seizing my throat. I suddenly remembered everything. I had dropped my sack after seeing the giant and had run without realizing it.

I looked up, my eyes growing wet as my vision blurred. The sky was gathering clouds and growing darker. Soon there would be an even mantle of deep blue fading into a shadeless black.

I could not go back now. Climbing in darkness was a sure way to break my neck. I had to wait for the morning.

The thought of going back scared me, but I could not leave my father's gift behind.

It was my guardian and represented all I had left of my family.

I couldn't lose it.

3

A FLAME WITH MANY NAMES

My father used to say there are three ways a man can make a fool of himself: by not keeping his promise, by drinking more than his stomach can handle, and by trying to do more than one thing at the same time.

That was why I kept my mind on the climbing, trying not to think about anything else while moving upward.

It was hard. The ache in my leg had gotten worse in the night, and now only sheer determination kept me going.

The sun was a blinding sphere a quarter of the way toward its zenith. I had set out for the peaks when the light had been nothing but a narrow disk of faint yellow pressed on the horizon.

I wanted to get back what was mine. I felt naked without it. I felt damned.

I learned long ago that people attach part of themselves to objects with a history that speaks to them. When the bond is forged, they treat something as simple as a piece of shaped rock as part of themselves. My father's gift was that to me. A third hand. A pumping heart. A part of my body I could not do without.

I had learned to treasure things from my father, who was famous for his craftsmanship. Everyone who met him said he had a unique gift for breathing life into objects.

It was true. My father had been skilled in many arts, but the first thing I remembered him for was his passion for traveling. He never stayed in one place for more than a few years and had served in the courts of many kings and sovereigns in his long life. He prided himself on being a mathematician and an architect, but his true calling had always been sculpture. And it showed. Many of his works still embellish the halls of princes and kings.

When my mother died, he made a statuette depicting her and gave it to me. He said it contained her last breath.

The sculpture was smaller than my palm, but it was one of his best works. He had admitted this himself. When I asked him why, he said, "It's because I put part of my soul in it."

That simple object symbolized the memory of both my parents, and there was nothing more valuable to me.

The sun climbed up the sky as I scrambled my way up the mountain.

By the time I reached the platform where I had found the giant, I could barely walk and my leg was pulsing with pain.

"Greetings, child of humankind."

I started. The giant was standing a few feet from the cliff, his back turned to me. He was taller than I had expected, over fifteen feet from head to toe, and his slate-gray skin made him look like a human-shaped pillar. He seemed to be looking intently at something on his barrel-sized palm. I gasped when I realized he was holding my statuette.

"Please," I said, clasping my hands together. "That statue is valuable to me. Don't break it."

"Break it?" The giant's voice was a low rumble, like a stone falling from a cliff. "Why would I want to break it? It's beautiful." He studied the sculpture for a few more seconds before turning to face me, his eyes blazing red. "I was wondering if you would come back for your things." He showed me his other hand, in which he held my travel sack.

I nodded awkwardly, raised an arm and then let it fall to my side. I looked from the giant to my travel sack, my eyes wide and darting.

"Well, then." He put the statuette inside the bag and held it out to me. "Take them."

I didn't move. A part of me was begging to leave, but I couldn't. I needed to get back my father's gift. I moved forward, my legs shaking.

"You're afraid of me." The giant frowned. "Don't be. I mean you no harm."

I didn't believe him. That colossal being frightened me. The closer I got to him, the more I realized his skin glowed, emanating an aura as blue-gray as his chains.

Eventually, I was just a few feet away from him. I glanced at the chains, well aware that they were stretched as far as possible. If I got any closer, the giant could seize me.

He seemed to sense my hesitation. "I understand," he said. He put the sack on the ground, then turned and went as far from me as the platform would allow. "Go on," he said, signaling for me to pick up the sack. "Now you can take it."

I snatched my things and backed away with a comical half-jump.

"There," the giant said, smiling. "Nothing better than to find what is believed to be lost; it's when the things we took for granted become real treasures."

I rummaged inside my travel sack and was relieved to find everything was still there. I stared at the giant, who had maintained his position on the opposite side of the platform.

"Is there something else you're looking for?" the giant asked.

I shifted, glanced at my bag. "N-no," I said. "Everything is in here."

"I'm glad to know that."

I put the travel sack over my shoulder and peeked back at the path that would lead me down and off the mountain. I didn't move, though. Instead, I studied the giant, who still had the friendly smile on his face.

The creature seemed harmless, if one didn't count his size as threatening, but he could just be pretending. Those chains looked strong enough, but I could not be completely sure. I wet my lips and maintained my position.

I had questions, many of them. Who was he? Who chained him in this remote place, and why? What was he—

"A fine work of art," the giant said, breaking my reverie.

"What?" I snapped back to attention.

The giant gestured toward my bag. "The statuette. Who made it?"

I pulled out my father's gift and looked at it. "My father," I said. "My father made it."

"He must be a skilled craftsman," the giant mused. "The smallest works are the hardest ones to get right. Proportions are difficult to maintain, and details become tricky." He closed his eyes and inhaled sharply. His hands moved in front of him, as though pinching something with his fingers. "Any mistake multiplies a hundredfold when crafting objects in a smaller scale." He opened his eyes and looked at the statuette as if the conversation had been between the two of them. "Who is she? The woman?"

I put the statuette back in the sack. "She was my mother. My father made this token as a gift, something to remember the both of them."

"Ah." The giant nodded thoughtfully. "You're wise to keep that gift close, traveler. One is never truly dead if remembered."

I cleared my throat, marveling at the conversation I was having with this giant, still wondering whether or not to leave.

"I can see you have questions of your own," the giant said, bobbing his head as if to invite me to talk. "Don't be afraid. Ask away."

"Are you a sculpture?" The words came out in a rush. It was a stupid question; I knew it the moment I uttered it. But the giant didn't seem to think that way.

"I guess I am, at that," he said. "A particular sort, you might say." He brushed the upper part of his abdomen absentmindedly. Only then I remembered that he'd had a deep wound pouring white blood just the day before. I blinked. Where had it gone?

"Yesterday—" I cut myself off. The sack's weight was taxing my leg. I put it on the ground and then resumed talking. "Yesterday you were wounded. You had a long gash on your side. I thought ... I thought you were dying."

The giant nodded gravely. "Yes." He studied the now smooth and blood-free skin. "I don't doubt you thought that."

"But that wound ... I mean, now you look fine."

The giant's smile turned sour. He gazed at the sky, his eyes searching for something. "For now," he said, his voice weary.

I waited for him to say something else, but time passed and the giant still looked up, his red eyes scanning the clouds. It seemed like he had completely forgotten about me.

"Who are you?" I asked.

The giant turned. He blinked, as if surprised I was still there. "Well," he said, his hands on his hips. "What do you see when you look at me?"

"I see a giant."

"Then you have your answer. I am a giant."

"People think you are a demon."

"Do they?"

"Yes," I said. "There is a village a few hours away from here." I pointed vaguely toward the south. "They said your screams date back several generations."

The giant bobbed his head twice. "They are right. I've been here for a long time."

I searched for another question, something that could make me understand more about this being, but all I could come up with was, "What's your name?"

The giant didn't answer immediately. This time he looked west, toward the horizon. It was as if he was trying to make sure of something. Then his eyes went back to me. "I have been called many names by mortals and gods: The Great Trickster, Forethought, Lord of Shadows and Bringer of Fire. I guess you can pick one of them."

"I see." I suddenly realized the colossal being was studying me with the same mixture of interest and amazement I was showing. That surprised me. It looked as if, for him, *I* was the fascinating creature standing on the platform.

I wiped my sweaty palms on my tunic, did my best to ignore his blazing eyes and asked, "Well, what do you call yourself?"

The giant folded his massive arms in front of his chest. "Prometheus," he replied. "That is the name I was born with."

"Then this is what I'll call you."

"And what is your name, traveler?"

"Zid, son of Xhoroast."

"Ah," the giant smirked. "The Fates have a peculiar sense of humor, don't they?" He said that as if he was talking to an invisible audience. "Zid means *truth* in the lost language of Ashur."

I jerked my head back, taken aback by the comment. "That's true. How do you know that?"

"The mighty god Ashur was a good friend of mine before his demise," Prometheus said. "I liked him. He always loved to sing and laugh and drink. He reminded me of the sun always rising, reluctant to give way to the darkness."

I scratched my head. "Wait a second. You're saying you knew the Assyrian winged sun-god?"

"By name and intention," Prometheus said proudly. "Like only a true friend can. He had several names; Ashur was only one of them."

I stood transfixed. This giant was saying he knew one of the greatest gods of the Mesopotamian Empire, now little more than a legend. "What's your relation to Ashur?"

"We were peers, and many times shared meat and mead at his heavenly halls."

"And you said he died?"

"In a way," Prometheus said, nodding slowly. "People stopped believing in him, replacing him with new beliefs, giving strength to them instead."

I felt my leg throbbing. I clenched my teeth and did my best to ignore it. "Are you a god yourself, Prometheus?"

The giant raised an eyebrow. He pondered the question for a while. Then he said, "I am a Titan."

"A Titan," I repeated. "I don't know that word."

"I am the descendant of a breed of giants that saw the making of the world. I never thought of myself as a god, but there are many who would call me that."

In retrospect, I now know it was at that moment that a simple itch to satiate my curiosity turned into something entirely different. I was no longer curious. I *needed* to know why this giant had been chained to a rock. And so I asked him.

"Why?" Prometheus echoed my question, seemed amused by it. "Well, opinions differ on the matter. If you ask my jailor, he'd tell you it's because I'm a rebel and a traitor."

"Who is that?" I asked. "Your jailor?"

"The royal son of Cronus," Prometheus said, his eyes narrowing. "Zeus himself." He looked at me. "Do you know the name?"

"Yes," I said. I had heard the name many times while traveling in the west. "He's a deity worshipped by the people who call themselves Hellenes. They refer to him as the God of Thunder."

Prometheus nodded. "Among many other names."

"What brought his wrath upon you?" Now that I had my first answers, more questions started surfacing. My leg was hurting, but I could not stop now. "Did he chain you because you killed somebody?"

The giant laughed a bitter laugh. "On the contrary," he said. "He chained me because I gave life."

"I don't understand."

"It's a long story, Zid," Prometheus said, the smile now wiped off his face as his eyes gazed on the horizon. "One I don't care to relate."

"They say long stories are the most meaningful ones."

Prometheus turned to regard me. "Who says that?"

"People with time to listen."

This time the giant's smile had mirth in it. "Tell me," he said, "how did you find me?"

"I heard a story from a nomad as I was traveling this region," I explained. "The 'shadow demon,' he and other folks called you. They talked of your screams at noon, and the story made me curious. I wanted to find out if you were real."

"Why?"

I shrugged. "Why not?"

Prometheus studied me. "Zid," he repeated my name, as if giving it a whole new meaning. "It looks like yours is a curious fate. A man bound to the meaning of his own name; a rare thing indeed. You are right. I have been here for a very long time. Many men must have heard my screams through all these years. I don't doubt they had questions, but they had no will to find an answer. None came."

I widened my eyes. "No one?"

"You are the first to brave the mountain and to find me. I know why. The truth is a gem few people seek, for its brightness can make a man blind. Most men will live until the end of their days in the familiarity of the darkness, even though it keeps them from the many blessings of the light. Curiosity is a gift one cannot give. Not even I. It is as precious as the statuette you're holding."

"I don't—" A sharp pain knocked the breath out of me. My leg failed me and I collapsed on the hard ground. A dull ache started radiating from my old wound. I had been a fool. I had ignored the signal my body had been giving me for too long.

"Are you ill?" Prometheus offered his hand and I took it. With the giant's help I was able to sit on a rock and wait out the wave of pain.

"Your face has turned as gray as the mountain." Prometheus's voice carried concern. "What is troubling you?"

"It's nothing," I said between clenched teeth. "Just an old scar that bothers me from time to time."

"Old scar," Prometheus repeated. "I see. Well, you should go back to where you come from before it gets worse. This is not a good place to have one of those seizures."

"Yes," I admitted with reluctance. I took a swig from my canteen and drank some spiced wine. "I think you are right."

"Why don't you climb down from this side?" Prometheus suggested, pointing to a depression of the platform. "There are more footholds here, and the descent is not as harsh. You can almost hop your way down."

I looked to where the Titan was pointing. He was right. That mountainside looked much easier to navigate from there.

"I will be back tomorrow," I said. "I have more questions."

"Questions only bring more questions," Prometheus said. "A seeker of knowledge should have learned that a long time ago."

"Still," I said, "I will come back tomorrow."

"I cannot stop you from visiting. But if you come back, do it in the morning, before noon. That is the only condition that I put upon you, but it is one I expect you to follow. Give me your word."

"Why before noon?"

Prometheus raised a hand. "That's a question for another day, Zid. You should move on before that leg of yours becomes useless."

"I ... I ..." I set my jaw. The Titan was right. "Very well. You have my word." I started down the mountain.

"One more thing."

I stopped and looked back at the giant.

"When you come back," Prometheus said, "bring clay and water with you."

"What?" I said, puzzled. "Clay and water? Why?"

"Because I might do something for that old scar of yours."

4

A MIRACLE OF CLAY

I headed back to the village, favoring my right leg. It took me almost twice as long as before, but I made it.

As always, I heard Prometheus's scream at noon. I was still a couple of hours away from the village when it happened, the sun a fiery eye that stifled the valley with a hot blanket of wet air, but I turned and wondered: What happened to the Titan at noon? What could make a god scream so? The screams lingered in the air for a long while before fading away into silence.

This time, no one looked at me when I approached the village square. People walked about minding their own business and didn't even glance in my direction. It was as if I didn't exist. If they had had any interest in my quest, it had disappeared.

I spent the evening in the old man's hut, drinking spiced wine and grinding my teeth.

When the day cooled, I went out to buy food and herbs. The village market was small and poorly stocked. I needed to find something to deal with the pain, but the market had none of the things I required, so I had to make do with what the vendors sold. I bought native herbs and roots that the village's herbalist told me could be boiled into a remedy for the pain, and some spices for my wine. Food-wise, the market offered mostly old barley bread, dried meat and overripe fruits. I traded a small pearl from the Ionian

Sea for a round loaf of bread as hard as stone and for a piece of dark yellow cheese that smelled like a wet goat. On my way back to the hut, I found the girl with blond hair tossing scraps of food to a small dog. The poor beast looked on the brink of starvation. The girl was holding a long wooden rod and used it to tap the ground as if following a rhythm.

"Hello," I said to her.

The dog snarled at me, his ears pressed on his narrow head.

"Be good, Xashon," the girl said, patting the dog's back. "He's not a wicked person. He's just weird." She glanced at my leg and pointed at it with her staff. "Why do you walk so?"

I leaned on a nearby wall to give my leg respite. "I had an accident years ago," I sighed. "My leg reminds me of that every time it can."

"What happened?"

"Well." I scratched my chin and smirked. "Do you feel like listening to another story?"

"Sure," the girl shrugged. "You're a decent storyteller."

"Decent?" I frowned. "Child, you make it sound as if I have a lot of competition." I gazed around. A couple of pigs were grunting in a pool made of dark water, mud and their own dung. "How many storytellers do you get around here?"

"Not very many," the girl admitted. "But I dream very interesting stories. I've got a lot of imagination, you know? Still, I like to listen to what others have to offer. Go on. I'm listening."

I could not help but smile at her smugness. I decided I liked her. "Well," I said, looking up as I summoned the past event. "Once upon a time, I was part of an expedition in a jungle south of Aryavarta. I was looking for a tablet that some said the many-armed goddess of wisdom, Saraswati, had written. Unfortunately, the expedition turned sour. A lion came from nowhere and killed half of the members of my team before being slain. The beast wounded my leg while I was trying to drive it away."

"Can I see it?" the girl asked. "Your wound?"

"Sure." I lifted my ankle-length tunic and showed her my wound. There was a long, thick portion of dark pink tissue where the scar had formed. The patch of flesh didn't seem to belong with the rest of my leg. It was ugly, but it was better than having no leg. "The beast has damaged the muscle," I said. "It could have been much worse. I was lucky enough that the healer of the expedition was extremely talented."

"Was he?" the girl chimed in.

"Yes," I said. "He fixed my leg with stitches and a very effective unguent."

"Good for you! Tell me," she said, getting closer to inspect the huge scar, "does it hurt?"

"Not always. Sometimes I'm barely aware of the pain."

The girl gave me a curt nod. "Did you find the tablet you were looking for?"

"Yes. Well, part of it, at least."

"What do you mean?"

"It turned out the tablet was broken. The missing part was never retrieved."

"I see. What was written in the half you found?"

"A story about the secret of living a fulfilled life."

"And what was the secret?"

I crossed my arms and smiled. "Unfortunately, the secret would be revealed in the missing part."

"Oh," the girl groaned. "You must have been disappointed."

"Not really. I'm convinced the tablet hinted what the secret might have been."

"And?" the girl asked. "What do you think it was?"

I stared at my leg, my eyes lost in thought. "I think there wasn't a second part of the tablet," I said.

"I don't understand." The girl was scratching the dog's ears. "What do you mean there wasn't a second part?"

"I think whoever put the tablet there didn't leave knowledge, but a riddle. And I think the answer was obvious: there are as many second parts as there are people."

The dog barked. He lolled his tongue and licked his mistress's hand.

The girl showed a smile that could have used a few more teeth. "I see," she said. "Was it worth it? Almost losing your leg over the knowledge?"

I looked at my scar, remembering the pain I felt and balancing it against the thrill of finding the tablet. "I like to think so," I said.

The girl glanced at the sweat that gathered on my forehead. Even though I was leaning on the wall, it was becoming increasingly difficult to stand.

"You don't look well," she said.

"I'll be all right," was my reply. "I just need to rest." I touched my scar. It was hot and an angry red.

She walked up to me. "Take this," she said, offering me her staff. "I can make another for myself."

I looked at the long stick. "Are you sure?" I asked.

The girl nodded.

"Well, thank you." I weighed the staff in my hand. It was rough but sturdy. "I owe you."

"You owe me nothing," the girl said with a smirk. "I liked your story. But I don't think you're right."

I looked at her, puzzled. "About what?"

"About the tablet," she said. "I think part of you is still looking for the second half."

I studied her, not knowing what to say.

"Come on, sorry-face," the girl said to her dog, clapping her hands. "Time to go."

The dog barked again and the both of them dashed away.

I looked at the girl and the dog disappearing behind one of the wider buildings. "What an odd child," I said to myself. I turned and headed back to my hut.

The girl's staff helped me distribute my weight better, and once back in my temporary shelter I made a draught out of the herbs and roots I bought in the market. That would help to speed up the recovery, but I knew that the best remedy was rest. And so I lay down and waited out the pain.

I barely slept that night. When I managed to close my eyes and find some rest, my dreams were besieged by dark thoughts.

Once again, my curiosity had brought me pain, but this time it was different. I had uncovered many mysteries and secrets in the past, but nothing like this Titan who called himself Prometheus. I had traveled into the lost caves of Purat, near the Buranuna River, and found paintings believed to be thousands of years old, made by men who shared the earth with monsters the size of palaces. I had witnessed the weather playing tricks with the minds of travelers venturing in the Egyptian desert, creating illusions of shapes and colors no one could explain. I had experienced a dozen different types of storms during one of the many travels I had undergone by sea, and in between them, I had seen Krakens breaking the sea with waves so high they could have swallowed a ship. I had stood in front of squat dragons without wings on one of the islands of the sharp-eyed folk in the Far East, and I had faced a tusked monster in the humid region of the Southeast, lapped by the river Síndhu.

But never had I spoken with a god.

I had grown used to the idea that the more I traveled, the more I would see the world as a mundane place with nothing new to offer.

I was wrong. The world is a shifting story whose twists you'll never see coming.

The next day, I woke up groggy and weak. The draught had dulled the pain, but had also made my leg as stiff as a wooden board. I grasped my staff and slowly made my way out. I sighed as I stared at the sky. It was already well into the afternoon, the sun long past his zenith. I cursed under my breath. I had missed my chance of speaking with Prometheus.

I looked at the peaks, wondering if the giant was waiting for me, as eager as I was, or if he didn't care at all.

I went back inside the hut, doing my best to ignore something that had been nagging at me since yesterday.

Was it worth it?

The girl's question made me angry. Of course it was. I was a discoverer, just like my father. I looked for answers to humankind's questions.

Your father wasn't a cripple, said a voice inside me. *He could sprint like a deer until the last day of his life. You are half his age and can barely stand.*

You should quit.

I clenched my jaw and did my best to ignore the taste of bile in the back of my mouth.

～

IT TOOK me two days to recover.

I went to the market each day, more to kill time than out of necessity. While browsing among the shops, I found an old lady selling pottery. She had a small stand where she exhibited some of her works: cups, food containers and plates—plain things that showed no real skill. I remembered what Prometheus had told me last time I saw him, so I approached the woman and asked her if she had any clay to spare.

She did. I offered her pearls and coins, as I had done with most of the other villagers, but she shook her head and gave me the clay, a warm smile plumping her already round cheeks.

"You brave man," she said in an accent I could not recognize. "You look for truth in the shadow." She glanced around at the people passing by, and sniffed. "These other men? All cowards. They hide in their homes, their heads low. You take this, and may good fortune be with you."

She wrapped the reddish matter in fresh, waxy leaves, and I put her gift in my travel sack. I thanked her and went on my way.

I should have rested another day before traveling again, but I could not bear to wait any longer.

I left the village the next morning, the staff from the girl scoring with a thud each step I took.

For the entire journey, I glanced at my leg with worry. I was eager to get to the chained god but afraid my leg would fail me once again.

I had lied to the girl when she asked about my leg. My wound was not getting any better. Every travel made it worse. Each time, I needed more days to recover, and the pain I suffered was crueler.

A part of me knew that my days as a traveler were numbered. Maybe that was why I pushed myself so hard. I wanted to get the most out of those years, while I was still young. The thought of being forced into a bed for the rest of my life scared me.

I pushed those thoughts aside and kept walking.

I arrived at my destination two hours before noon. I found Prometheus sitting crossed-legged.

"Ah, Zid," the Titan said, glancing at me over his shoulder while sliding a big round stone on the ground, his expression thoughtful. "I was beginning to think you had found more interesting shadows to seek."

I squinted and noticed narrow lines marked on the portion of the platform right in front of the giant. They were sculpted into the stone. Pieces with various shapes sat on the squares formed by the intersections of the lines. It looked like the Titan was playing some kind of board game.

I rested my back on a rock shaped like a pillar, the hand that wasn't holding the staff busy rubbing my sore leg. "Pressing necessities kept me," I said.

"Hmm." The Titan's eyes lingered on my staff. "Your leg?"

I let my silence be the answer I didn't want to offer.

Prometheus dusted his hands. His chains rattled as he rose. "Did you bring what I asked?"

I left the staff on the ground and rummaged inside my travel sack. I took out the clay and the waterskin. I gave both to the giant.

He unwrapped the clay from the leaves and studied the reddish block, turning it in his hands. "Come sit over here," he said, pointing to a nearby rock that resembled a fallen tree trunk.

I trudged toward the rock and sat.

"Uncover your leg," Prometheus ordered.

When I pulled up my tunic, the giant studied the long scar that ran from my knee to my quadriceps. He gently pressed his index finger on it.

I winced.

"Does it hurt more when I push or when I release the pressure?"

"When you push," I grimaced.

"Hmm." Prometheus scratched his bald head. "Then the answer is adding."

"Adding?" I echoed. "Adding what?"

The Titan didn't answer. He poured water over the brick, and when the material had become malleable he started shaping it, pushing and flexing it with his fingers. Once he had a long, thin spread of red clay, he pressed it on my leg, shaping it until it covered all of my quadriceps. The clay was damp and warm against my skin.

"What are you doing?" I asked him.

"We're both going to find out."

I looked at him, not happy with that answer. "What do you mean?"

Prometheus sighed. "It's been a long time since I practiced the *Art*," he said, stressing the word *art* as if it meant more than the word itself. "I should also add that these chains wither most of my powers." He eyed the heavy metal links binding him to the mountain. "That means I'm not sure I can fix your leg."

I blinked. "So that's what you're doing? You're trying to fix my leg?"

"Well," he said, frowning. "I thought that was plain enough."

"What if it doesn't work?"

"In that case," he said, "we'll have wasted some good clay. Now be quiet. I need to focus."

Prometheus whispered words I could not understand. Somehow, his voice made me sleepy. I closed my eyes and dozed off.

"It's done."

I yawned and opened my eyelids slowly. The clay had disappeared from my leg.

"How ... where ..." I trailed off, feeling disoriented. I was sure my leg had been covered by the reddish matter just a few seconds before, but now there was nothing.

"Stand," Prometheus said.

"Stand?" I looked at the staff on the ground. "Well, I need my staff to—"

"Leave it. I want you to stand by yourself."

I did nothing to hide my worry. "I'm not sure it's a good idea," I said. "It hurt the last time I tried to put weight on it."

"I know," Prometheus said. "I'm asking you to trust me."

"I ... well, as you wish." I pushed myself up slowly. The leg felt very cold, as though it had been buried in snow.

"Don't favor your weak leg," Prometheus warned me. "Distribute your weight evenly."

I groaned, but I did as the Titan asked me. Only then did I realize that the scar had disappeared.

"My scar!" I exclaimed. "It's gone!"

"Yes, yes," Prometheus said dismissively. "What about the pain? Do you feel any?"

I looked down at my leg. "No," I said, a wild smile blossoming on my face. "I ... I don't feel anything."

"Now stand solely on your right leg," Prometheus ordered.

Gingerly, I redistributed my entire weight to my faulty leg. No ache, no discomfort of any kind. The pain was gone, like it had never existed. I stared at my leg as if it wasn't my own.

"How did you do that?" I asked Prometheus as I started walking up and down the platform, testing my healed leg.

"A good sculptor remembers the making of his masterpiece," Prometheus said, "and how to fix it when time or ill fortune chips away its frame. I was right in fearing those chains had stripped my powers. But luckily, they did nothing to my skills." He looked at his hands, relief flooding his face. "Those, at least, remain."

I stopped walking. "Wait a second." I stared at him, barely breathing. "Did you say, 'the making of your masterpiece'?"

"Yes," the Titan admitted. "That's what I said."

I snorted. "You mean to say that you made *me*?"

"Don't be ridiculous." The giant chuckled. "Your parents made you. But your ancestors ... well, they didn't sprout from the ground. They were made with clay."

My hands dropped to my sides. "You mean ... you're saying you made the first members of humankind?"

The long chain that bound him to the rock clattered when Prometheus nodded. "Yes. That is a part of the story that ends with me chained to this mountain."

I expected him to add more, but Prometheus simply stared at his hands, letting the howling of the wind fill the silence.

I slowly walked toward him, my desire to know more growing at every step. "Tell me the story," I said. "Please."

The Titan looked abashed. "It's a dark part of my past, Zid. Why do you wish to know it?"

"It would help me understand you better."

Prometheus regarded me with scorn. "A seeker of truth to the very core. Why wouldn't you want to know, after all? That's all I am to you, hmm? A puzzle wrapped in a mystery, waiting to be solved.

Nothing more than another chapter in the book of your adventures."

The shift in Prometheus's tone, suddenly so harsh and threatening, stilled my heartbeat for half a second. "No," I mumbled, my voice shaky. "Listen. I … I didn't mean to—"

Prometheus walked up to me until the chains stopped him. "You know why secrets are held so dear by gods and men? It's because they are ashamed of them, and they can do nothing but hide them further and further inside their souls. By holding so close the things no one else knows, they allow these secrets to pollute them. I am a hostage to many secrets, Zid, son of Xhoroast, some of them so dangerous they could unmake the world. I've seen things the tale of which could make a man mad and turn his heart into ashes. I've seen the world changed into many worlds with the currency of blood. You're asking me to unveil some of that darkness as a farmer is asked to feed peas to pigs. You should understand something, seeker of truth: Sometimes, ignorance is a blessing."

"I'm sorry," I said, my eyes cast down. "I shouldn't have asked. You have been kind with me, and I repaid you with impertinence and my egoistic need to know." I picked up my travel sack and the staff, and I made to go. "Thank you for healing my leg. I won't bother you any longer." I started walking away.

"Wait." Prometheus rubbed his neck. His eyes had lost much of their brightness. "I'm the one who should apologize." He reached out as if to pat my shoulder but then pulled back. "It's been too long since I spoke with a mortal. I forgot so many things about you. There was a time when I appreciated curiosity. In fact, I rewarded it. And look at me now. Afraid of my own shadow."

I searched for something wise to say, but I couldn't come up with anything that seemed appropriate. Only a story came to me, and I shared it with Prometheus. "I understand what you mean. When I was ten, I had nightmares almost every night. I knew I wasn't to disturb my parents' sleep, for they both worked hard in the day, and so I spent my nights crying in the darkness. One day my cries woke my mother.

"What are those tears, son of my heart?" she asked, sitting beside me.

"Mother, I cannot sleep," I answered between sobs. "Nightmares with ghosts are waiting for me. They will swallow me whole if I close my eyes."

She smiled then and wiped the tears off my cheeks. "I'll tell you a secret," she said. "Something that will help you sleep."

I looked at her, clinging to her arm as if it were the last thing that would keep me from falling down a cliff. "What is it, mother? Please, tell me. I'm so scared!"

She brushed my sweaty hair and said, "Hearth of my soul, hear me: there's no better way to chase away ghosts than to summon them and stare in their eyes."

I smiled at the memory as my eyes went back to Prometheus. "The next night, when I felt chased by a ghost, I remembered my mother's words. I turned and looked at my worst fear. You know what I found? Nothing but smoke."

A smile took over Prometheus' face. "Your mother was a wise woman. You are right. There is no reason not to answer your question, other than my fear of reviving my fear. I will tell you the story." Prometheus glanced at the Sun. "Or at least, a version of the story. We still have some time left."

The Titan lifted both hands and stepped up to me, his fingers mere inches from my head.

"What are you doing?" I glanced warily at his outstretched hands as I backed away.

"Words can only go so far," Prometheus smiled reassuringly. "Some of the things I'll tell you are difficult to grasp for a mortal mind. It will be easier if I can show you images as well. Fear not. It won't hurt you."

I hesitated, my body stiffening and going still. I looked at the giant's hands, so massive they could have crushed a stone in a heartbeat.

"Trust me, Zid," the Titan said, his voice carrying the soothing familiarity of a friend's promise. "This will give you the knowledge you seek in the purest form."

I swallowed, searched the giant's blazing eyes and found nothing but kindness. I gathered my courage and nodded. "Very well." I stepped forward, allowing him to place both hands close to my head. "I'm ready."

"Good." Prometheus closed his eyes and inhaled deeply. "Sit down, and let my voice be your guide. Your next journey is about to begin."

This time I kept my questions to myself and just sat down on the cold ground, listening without interrupting as Prometheus's voice rolled on, unveiling the tale before us.

5

THE MAKING OF HUMANKIND

"There never was peace in creation. Humankind has forged many ways of telling the same tale, the story of the making of the world. Most of these accounts try to give sense to something no mortal will ever truly grasp. This is how everything started: A spark of energy at the edge of eternity, bound with a shard of matter, giving birth to time and space in a glorious dance of fire. That was the beginning from which everything else originated. We will never know the *why*, only the *how*."

I was only half-aware of Prometheus's voice as the Titan related the tale. My mind was swallowed by what was all around me: darkness and silence.

Then, something happened, something I can only describe as a black star exploding in the vastness of nothing, causing dark waves to cross leagues and leagues of space in the blink of an eye. I opened my mouth, my mind overwhelmed by a sight my wildest dream could not have created. Prometheus' voice returned, and I followed it like a moth chasing the only source of light in a world swallowed by night.

"The outcome was a rough, initial version of the cosmos that led to the rise of the Great Lord Chaos, the everlasting god who made all the other deities possible."

I saw it. I say *it* because Chaos had no gender, no color, no shape. Nothing but vastness and power defined it. It was as if a spark of the initial clash of matter and energy had become sentient somehow and was now moving of its own accord, spawning a smaller version of itself, also equipped with a keen awareness of the universe.

"From the Great Lord Chaos sprouted the Primordial gods: Gaia, Tartarus, Eros, Erebus, Hemera and Nyx, the makers of the world and of the underworld. They gave balance to the matter Chaos was born from; they distributed names among things and gave clear boundaries to creation. It was the Primordial gods who gave life to us, the Titans, born by Mother Gaia and Father Uranus, deities with powers able not only to shape the world but also the stars."

Prometheus paused, and I saw the darkness slowly replaced by a pulsing light. It came from everywhere and nowhere and gave colors and shapes to the world. Our world. It was a primitive version of our home, a vast desert occasionally dotted by colossal mountains, where storms made of fire and thunder scoured the land. But things were changing. A silent force was working swiftly to change the face of the world. I saw mountains leveled in the blink of an eye to make room for valleys, water rushing into the dry, shallow scars of the earth to form the first rivers and lakes, and specks of green sprouting east and west, like flowers in a well-tended garden.

I felt Prometheus's gentle pull, directing my gaze closer to the land, toward shapes that were moving in all directions. They were giants, some as big as palaces, their eyes the color of the sun. Their resemblance to Prometheus was striking. I realized they were the architects building our world from the ground up. They were the ones making space for all the life that would soon populate every land and sea.

"I and my brothers and sisters further shaped the earth to make it beautiful, thriving with life." Prometheus's voice resonated from inside and outside of me, like an omniscient narrator telling the story of creation to one of his characters. "Stability was maintained for a while, but transformation was bound to happen again, and happen it did. Cronus, one of the first Titans, challenged his father, Uranus, because the elder god had been consumed by a lust for power, which made him cast Gaia's children into the deep abyss of Tartarus."

Suddenly, I saw black lightning tearing apart a blood-red sky. Earthquakes fractured the land as two massive beings wrestled each other for dominion over creation. Then, in the boundary between earth and sky, I saw a blinding light, followed by an earth-shaking roar. The sky shattered in a million tiny pieces, the ocean started boiling, and then a deep silence followed. Prometheus's tale resumed.

"Cronus rallied the Titans to fight against his father and won by castrating Uranus with a stone sickle, throwing his father's severed genitals into the ocean. With the fall of Uranus, creation was handed over to the Titans. Cronus and his sister Rhea took the throne of the world as king and queen. We Titans call that period the Golden Age, because that time called for no rules or laws; everyone behaved with honor, and immorality was a far-fetched concept."

Prometheus spoke the truth. I saw nothing but beauty and peace, in a world restored of its balance after the war between Cronus and Uranus. The Titans were many, and multiplying quickly over land and sea. The entire cosmos became their dominion as they took the role of shepherds of creation.

I felt something tugging at my chest, a slight discomfort creeping up from my stomach. The feeling surprised me, for I had nothing but awe and marvel in my heart. It took me some time to realize that feeling wasn't mine. It was Prometheus's. Somehow, the link he created between us allowed me to also feel what he was feeling as he related the story. The Titan was growing uneasy, as if the following part of the tale might cast the very shadows he was afraid to unveil.

"The balance was not meant to last." Prometheus said these words as if unwilling, like a cow dragged out of the stable, sensing the destiny awaiting her in the slaughterhouse. "In time, Cronus changed. He became suspicious and wary of his own children when he learned that one of them would overthrow him, just as he had overthrown Uranus. So he took measures to ensure his reign would last."

The images Prometheus put in front of me were odd. I saw

Cronus snatch something from the hand of his spouse, then swallow it whole. I narrowed my eyes to try to make sense of what I was seeing. I just couldn't make out—

"He ate his own children." Prometheus's voice was quavering, revealing his own disgust and shame. I felt my own heart racing at the horror happening in front of me, a sudden coldness seizing my soul.

"Cronus devoured the goddess Demeter, Hera, Hestia and the gods Poseidon and Hades as soon as they were born to prevent the prophecy from coming to fruition. But Cronus's shameless act was not meant to last. Zeus, the youngest of his sons, escaped his father. In time, he grew strong and brave and managed to free his siblings from the Titan's stomach by giving him a special herb that made him disgorge them. Then, he led a new generation of gods who called themselves Olympians and waged war on the Titans."

Again I saw the world shaken by earthquakes. The sky turned black and the air grew heavy with the sound of battle. I saw the clash between the giants and the Olympians unfolding before me, the new gods battling the old ones with lightning bolts, fireballs and water storms, the Titans answering with earthquakes, hurricanes and waves of dark energy. Many fell on both sides, in a war that made the previous one seem like a meaningless squabble between children.

"Most of the Titans fought alongside Cronus," Prometheus explained, as he showed me the giant race hurling rocks and shards of dark energy against Zeus and his allies. "But some of us joined the Olympians. My brother Epimetheus and I were among them."

I saw a glimpse of Prometheus and Epimetheus side by side in the midst of that madness. They both carried long spears ending with a sharp diamond head, and a golden shield that could withstand the giant rocks of fire falling from the sky. Their skin was of a brilliant adamant blue so glorious it hurt to watch.

The brothers dodged the Titans' blows, moving swiftly and in deadly fashion against their own kin. The way they moved is hard to describe. They did everything in unison, like dancers rehearsing a well-known performance, like bodies answering to one mind; one would strike, while the other would stand to protect the both of them with the shield. They were a balanced unity of war, spreading havoc among their foes.

"After a decade of fierce war, the Titans were forced to bend the knees." Prometheus's voice accompanied the image of Zeus dragging a row of chained Titans in the deepest recesses of the earth. "Some were cast into the deeper regions of Tartarus, condemned to stay there for eternity. But not all. Cronus and a few Titans who had opposed Zeus more fiercely were condemned by the king of the Olympians to drink a draught called dystheos, made by Nyx, the Primordial deity of the night. The draught stripped the Titans of all their powers, leaving only their immortality. They were condemned to experience hunger and fatigue, as any common mortal. It's one of the worst punishments a god can suffer, the closest thing we can ever experience to death."

A new image dawned before me. The sun rose on a scarred land, but the air brought the promise of the future with it. A new order was about to rise from the ashes of war.

"The Titans who sided with Zeus were spared," Prometheus said. "To some, the Olympians gave prestigious places in the new order. My brother Epimetheus and I were two of them. Zeus entrusted us with the creation of a new generation of living creatures. My brother was to distribute the gifts of the gods among all beings living on earth, in air and in water. I was to create the first members of humankind. While my brother was distributing the gifts, I shaped the first humans out of clay, formed you in the images of the gods. I used all my skills and powers for your creation, because it had been foretold that you would be my greatest masterpiece. I endowed you with reason, a gift only the Primordials, the Titans and the Olympians had. In the beginning, Zeus looked at my work with interest. He knew I was one of the best minds among the Titans, and he was curious about what I would accomplish. However, when I showed the first human to Zeus, he was enraged. He didn't like the way you looked at him. Your eyes weren't downcast; there was no reverence in your voice when you addressed him, no fear. You stood in front of the greatest god as an equal."

Prometheus's voice faded. For a time, I didn't see anything but a thick blanket of fog enveloping the world. I blinked and looked around, searching for a shape amid that whiteness. There he was! A man, the first human being ever created, stood in front of me. He was taller than any man I had ever encountered—seven, maybe eight feet tall—but his features were rough, almost grotesque. The first of humankind had no hair, and his nose and ears were barely distinguishable from the rest of the smooth, shaved head. His eyes, ever-moving and filled with awareness, were the only things that looked human.

Zeus stood in front of the first of humankind, the god's sky-blue eyes narrowing as he studied the mortal, his forehead creased in a deep frown.

"My creation appalled the King of the Olympians," Prometheus said, and I could feel the tension in his voice. "He stormed into my laboratory, destroyed my instruments, and seized the clay I used to create you. He burned everything to the ground; then he ordered that humans were to be servants to the gods and made sure they needed his protection to survive. From that moment on, you would need the gods' blessing from the elements, and would rely on them for shelter. When you were hungry, you would need to pray to the gods not to starve. He degenerated my creation, made you dependent on Olympus, as worms on wet ground."

Prometheus showed me a group of people living in a cave. They walked naked on the rough ground, feeding on roots and berries and wild mushrooms. A thunderclap boomed from outside and the humans fell to their knees, closed their eyes and raised their arms, as if to fend off a blow.

"Zeus turned you into another amusement for the gods." Prometheus's voice was barely a whisper now, but I could feel the hate each word carried. "I saw the way the Olympians treated you, and every day a part of me died, until I decided to do something. When I had set my mind on creating you, my purpose had been one: to make a new race that had the potential of becoming gods through ingenuity and technique. I thought this new god, Zeus the cloud-gatherer, would be open-minded, but he saw my attempt at creating you as blasphemy. I was wrong about him. He was as bigoted as his father. Trusting him was a mistake I would never make again.

"I had a plan to make things right—and no fear of the consequences it would bring. I climbed Mount Olympus and stole the
sacred white fire from the workshop of the blacksmith god
Hephaestus. I brought the flame back to earth and gifted it to
humankind. With that flame, I gave humans not only heat but also
all the possibilities that come with civilization. I gave you the
power to harness nature for your own benefit, to dominate
creation rather than be dominated by it. I gave you the power of
the gods."

The next images Prometheus put in front of me were simple. I
saw the once-scared people crawling out of their cave and building
a fire. They gathered around it and started talking, making plans,
the future no longer a shadow ready to swallow them, but a treasure chest filled with possibilities.

"The first civilizations were born out of that fire." I felt pride in
the Titan's voice; the way his words rolled on reminded me of a
father watching his firstborn child taking his first steps. "Science,
war and art soon followed. For a time I was happy. I witnessed the
first human settlements rising in the east and in the west. I saw the
first tools created by humankind. The way you started shaping
nature to your will was ingenious and unexpected. You no longer
prayed to the gods for food. You went out and hunted it. You were
still a young race, prone to fail more times than I could count, but
you were quick to rise, to try something new, and to expand your
knowledge no matter the cost. That fire was all you needed to
become the master of your own fate."

Prometheus fed my mind with countless more images, so many
it was hard to keep track of them all. I saw a group of hunters
chasing a monstrous beast with fur as dark as a moonless night
and armed with long claws and tusks; a monster that had killed
countless of them before the Titan's gift was now nothing but a
form of prey that would feed and dress them. I saw fire burning a
forest to make room for human settlements. I saw tools made of
stones and wood and ore. And in between scenes of that genesis, I
saw angry lightning bolts, clouds amassing in the sky. I felt the
rage of the King of the Olympians as humanity multiplied, prospered and found its way in the world.

"My happiness didn't last for long." The Titan's voice broke the silence and all the images faded into an even blanket of mist. I saw Prometheus at the center of that whiteness, his eyes closed, his head bowed low. "When Zeus found out what I had done, his rage blackened the sky. But it was too late. He could not take the fire back, nor undo what I had done. A gift of a deity cannot be taken back easily, not even by Zeus."

Prometheus raised his massive hands, and a set of chains appeared around his wrists. The mist dispersed, and now I could see the mountain he was bound to. "For my transgression, Zeus chained me in this desolate region of the Caucasus, and left me here to rot. Sometimes I feel his eyes looking at me, basking in my misery."

Prometheus's eyes jerked open. They shone with fire. He lifted his head, looked at the sky with a fiery challenge. "Let him look," he said, his words a statement of defiance. "I would do it all over again."

6

LOSER'S GAME

Fragments of rocks rasped against the lifeless ground, blown by the wind coming from the north. A gust of chill air washed over me, and I shivered.

I emerged from the vision of the past as if pulled away by a gentle tugging. I looked around, blinked. I was still on the platform, but now I was standing. How much time had passed? To me, it felt like an eternity.

I found Prometheus in front of me, his hands clasped behind his back. The Titan had stopped talking, his eyes staring at nothing.

"For how long have you been here?" I asked, the words scratchy.

Prometheus's eyes were dull, lifeless. "Since the dawn of civilization."

"How many years is that?"

"Many." Prometheus shrugged. "I didn't keep count. I was never good at staring at the sand falling in the hourglass."

"And for how long will Zeus keep you chained?"

Prometheus's answer was as sharp as a razor. "For eternity."

That put a full stop to our conversation.

The Titan looked like he had been depleted of all his energy from relating his story. Every additional word seemed to tax him to the point of breaking.

I must admit, I was also wrapped in thought.

When the nomad told me the story of the shadow demon, I hadn't expected to find the maker of humankind. Prometheus's story was intertwined with the story of creation itself. It was humbling to be there, in front of this giant who had seen the making of the world and who had been made to pay for giving us a power meant only for the gods. Somehow, though, it also felt wrong.

I shifted my weight from one foot to the other, uncomfortably. An odd feeling seized me. Suddenly, I felt responsible for the punishment Prometheus was enduring.

"Your story moved me," I said, looking at the giant sideways. "I'm sorry for what happened to you. Is there ... is there anything I can do?"

I know my offer sounded meaningless, but I genuinely wanted to help Prometheus. It wasn't because he had healed my leg. After his story, I felt that I knew him better, as if the barrier that divided the two of us, a mortal and a god, had vanished.

The Titan curled the side of his mouth in a smirk. I thought I knew what his expression meant: What could a puny mortal like you do to help me?

"Forgive me," I added hastily. "I'm presuming too much. I shouldn't have said that."

"You want to do something for me?" Prometheus raised his arms, spread his hands. "But you did already." He leaned toward me. "You have been the best audience I ever had."

I looked at him, shaking my head slightly. "What?"

"I always enjoyed telling stories," Prometheus explained, his eyes summoning back the brightness they had lost when he related his story. "However, when I was surrounded by gods they would stop me or get bored and walk away. Their attention span is short, they get distracted easily, and words do not amuse them enough to keep them listening for long. Only my brother Epimetheus endured my tales. You are the first one besides him to listen until the very end."

"Prometheus, you gave me back my leg," I said, blinking. "I hardly think that listening to a story will repay that."

"Well." The Titan looked toward the portion of the platform

that had been smoothed out and turned into a game board. I could see it was a grid of sixty squares, arranged in six rows of ten, all carved shallowly on the ground. "I have always wanted someone to play with. You know, after a while it gets frustrating to be beaten by myself."

"Is that a game?"

"The finest I could come up with in lifetimes of isolation."

"What's it called?" I asked.

"Why, I don't know." Prometheus scratched his forehead. "I've never thought of giving it a name."

"Right. Why don't you teach me the rules?"

Prometheus motioned for me to sit across from him. Suddenly, he looked very excited.

"Look," he said, pointing at the game board. "Each stone is placed on a square. There are three kinds of stones: triangle, square and circle." He pointed to each different-shaped stone. There were two different sets, one light gray and the other black. "Any stone moves in the same fashion, but each one has a different role. Triangle eats square, circle is eaten by square, while circle eats triangle. Each player has one turn to move one piece. The pieces can only move diagonally on the board. And this is how you set the pieces."

Prometheus went on explaining the rules. The game was relatively simple to understand but not easy to play. It was based on the assumption that one player had to risk many of his pieces to conquer the rival's part of the board. There were many rules and exceptions that Prometheus explained to me. As I was playing, the Titan's invention reminded me a bit of Senet, a board game played in Egypt, although the board the Titan used was different and the pieces could do things the Egyptian version couldn't.

We played three games, and I lost all of them. Every time, I learned a bit more about the strategy behind this pastime, but really what kept me playing was seeing the Titan's face light up. It was as if a boy had been given a brand new toy and couldn't stop showing it to his friend.

"I like your style," Prometheus said as he was setting up the board to play the fourth game. "You are as unpredictable as the wind."

"Is that good?"

"Indeed. I never thought a mortal could play this well."

"I'll take that as a compliment."

After losing for the fourth time, my gaze lingered on the board, and something came to me.

"What happens if we draw?" I said. "The pieces are set to make that outcome not likely, but possible."

Prometheus produced a sound halfway between a gurgle and a chuckle. "If we draw," he said, "we both lose."

"Why lose?" I picked up one of the square-shaped stones and looked at it intently. "Couldn't we both win? Why do we both have to lose?"

Prometheus shrugged. "It just seemed more reflective of the real order of things. When both contenders don't get what they want, I call that losing. There is only victory or defeat. No place for middle ground."

We played another game, talking in between moves. I told Prometheus about the simple life of the villagers who lived a few hours away from him, and how little thought they gave his screams.

"I envy them," the Titan said, moving a circle-shaped stone and eating one of my triangles.

"You envy them?" I said, puzzled. "Why?"

"None of them are chained, for a start. They can go where they please, and their simple lives don't make them the target of divine punishment. Shall I continue?"

"No. I think you made your point."

I moved my piece and then looked at the chains binding Prometheus to the rock. "There is something you left out of the story," I said. "What happens to you at noon?"

Prometheus's face hardened. He slid a stone on the ground but didn't answer.

"The screams are yours," I pressed him. "Of that I'm sure."

"Yes," he said. "They are mine."

"It has something to do with the wound that magically heals?"

"Believe me, there is nothing magical. It's just another part of my punishment."

"Zeus's punishment," I said. "But it doesn't explain why you seem so afraid of—"

"Zid," the Titan dragged each letter of my name, as if they were made of lead. "That's enough."

I kept my fingers on the stone I was waiting to move. Prometheus's face was a mask that kept his emotions hidden, but I could see his hand growing unsteady as he moved a piece. "It's something I don't wish to talk about." He looked at me, his eyes two flames that flickered dangerously. "I have dispersed enough ghosts for one day. For that, I thank you, but I won't try my luck. Not today. Do you understand?"

"I understand," I said, offering no objections. Something had shifted inside the giant, and I could feel the tension hanging in the air. *Secrets*, Prometheus had called them, things that burned inside him. This one seemed hard to give up. "Forgive me," I added. "I didn't mean to intrude."

"There is nothing to forgive." Prometheus's expression softened. "I enjoy your company, Zid, and you are becoming good at this game. Your turn." He signaled me to move.

We played in silence for a few turns; then the Titan looked at me. "So," he said. "Now that you have played several times, what do you propose we call the game?"

"You want *me* to give it a name?"

"Why not?" Prometheus said. "Surprise me."

I looked at the game board, and at the different stones. Maybe something that had to do with the oddly shaped pieces? Perhaps something about the number of the squares that formed the game board? No. Nothing felt quite right.

I scratched my chin, and then something came to me. "This is the first game that I've played where both players can lose," I said. "I think 'Loser's Game' is befitting."

"Loser's Game?" Prometheus frowned. "It sounds foreboding."

"You don't like it."

"I find it peculiar," Prometheus admitted. "You see, when I was—"

A shrill sound shredded the silence, and we both looked up to the sky.

"Tartarus's black flames!" Prometheus rose, scattering the

stones as he did so. "The sun has reached its zenith. I'm a fool." He turned toward me. "You need to go. Now!"

"I—" I wanted to ask him to let me stay, but the giant's eyes were set on me. He didn't look like he was willing to discuss the subject, and I wasn't going to enrage a fifteen-foot-tall Titan.

"Very well." I quickly gathered my things. When I was done, I glanced at my leg, still marveling at the miracle that had happened. "I want to thank you again for—"

"Leave," the giant cut me off. "Now." His eyes were searching the sky as if the blue dome was about to fall on us.

I abandoned the platform and started climbing down the mountain. Then I heard something else: a series of high-pitched noises coming from the north. I stopped my descent and glanced at the platform.

I knew I had promised Prometheus to go, but my curiosity had got the better of me. This time I waited.

From my position, I could see Prometheus standing on the platform without being seen.

The high-pitched sound became a shrieking noise, like a thousand knives brushing on a bronze shield. A vast shadow descended from the sky, and something landed on the platform. I peeked from my position and looked at it.

A massive eagle as big as a horse was flapping wings large enough to cast a shadow on the mountain. Her plumage was as otherworldly as the rest of her body, a stark metallic brown that reminded me of bronze.

Before I could realize what was happening, the beast threw its full weight against Prometheus, and the Titan crashed hard on the mountainside. It all happened in a few heartbeats. Prometheus didn't fight back; he just wailed when the eagle tore his side with a beak the size of a man's forearm, her talons shimmering with the giant's white blood. Prometheus's scream was a bellowing cry of pain as the monstrous bird feasted on his liver, tearing it apart.

I covered my mouth, unable to do anything other than watch with horror the agony the Titan was going through, his shouts crushing my soul as the scene unfolded before my eyes.

A fragment of the rocky ledge I was clinging on fell with a noisy tumble. The eagle's head spun toward me, her nostrils tasting the air, her eyes searching for me. And it was those eyes that shredded the last remnant of my courage. They were elliptical, with thin, black, vertical pupils surrounded by a yellow-green eyeball.

I am ashamed to say this, but I ran away as fast as I could, leaving the eagle to feast on Prometheus's liver, not once looking back.

The villagers had it all wrong. The demon wasn't chained to the mountain. It came from the sky, and it had wings and feathers and eyes like a venomous snake.

7

A TRADING OF STORIES

That night, in the village, I moved like a ghost. The marvelous feeling of having my leg restored to its full health was spoiled by what I had seen.

I finally knew what the nature of Prometheus's punishment was. An eagle ate the Titan's liver every day, and every day the liver regrew, only to be eaten again. Hundreds, possibly thousands of years of that agony, and an eternity more to come.

I looked at my leg, feeling ashamed. With a single gesture, the Titan had ended years of torment and had given me back my mobility. For a traveler, that was everything. And all I could do for him was to run away like a mouse when he might have needed me.

I had never believed in destiny. My father told me that every man makes his own fortune, and that even the gods have no say over what a person might become. I believed in those words. But now, thinking of Prometheus's story, I was no longer so sure.

What if meeting the nomad hadn't been a chance encounter? What if I was destined to find Prometheus and help him regain his freedom? What if all my travels brought me to this moment?

I didn't know how a simple man like me could undo Zeus's punishment, but in that moment, something shifted inside me. I wouldn't leave these mountains until the Titan was free.

It sounded like a madman's resolution, but that was now my mission.

It was at that moment, while I was striding between the low buildings made of clay and soil, thinking about what I could do, that I ran into a group of hunters carrying furs and game they had probably hunted in the morning.

They all brought with them the same short bow that I had noticed other hunters carry.

Suddenly, an idea flashed in my mind. I raised my hand and called one of the hunters.

"Good man," I said. I took one of my gems and showed it to him. "How would you like to trade this for your bow?"

The hunter was more than happy to do the trade. No doubt he could fashion a similar bow in less than a day, while I did not understand how to make one.

I noticed that some of his arrows were painted red, and I asked him why. He said they drenched those with purplehead snake poison. After a few questions, I realized it was the same snake that had killed my horse. I traded a few of them for one of my oldest vests, and then I safely wrapped them in an old piece of cloth.

When the trade was done, I studied the weapon. It differed from any bow I had used. Shorter and sturdier, the string was tough to bend, but once the arrow was nocked and released, it would shoot far and true.

In my many travels I had often used a bow, mostly to hunt, but a few times to defend myself. I might not have been the best archer in the world, but I knew how to shoot an arrow to kill.

The next trip to Prometheus's prison took much less time than usual, and I was at the base of the Titan's mountain when noon was still several hours away.

I hid the bow in a cavity of the rock and climbed the rest of my way up to the platform.

I found Prometheus playing his game of stones. For a long time I maintained a distance and stood at the edge of the platform, motionless, looking at the giant's back. I was trying to decide the best way to tell him what I saw.

"Zid," the giant grunted. "Aren't you tired of staring at my back? What is troubling you?"

I walked up to him. "I saw the eagle, yesterday. I saw what it did to you."

Prometheus straightened up. He turned to regard me.

"I'm sorry," I said.

"Sorry?" Prometheus's red eyes were unblinking. "For what? For breaking your promise? Or sorry for me?"

"For both things."

Prometheus turned back to the game board and resumed playing. "At least now you know it's not something I enjoy relating. It does nothing to lift my mood."

"I can imagine that," I said. "How do you bear it?"

"As best I can." He moved a stone, then stared at the game board with his arms folded tightly against his chest. "You know, the worst part is not when the eagle comes. It's the waiting in between that's hard to endure."

He started resetting the pieces.

"Why the liver?" I asked him. "The eagle didn't seem interested in anything else when she attacked you."

Prometheus touched his abdomen absentmindedly. "For us Titans, the liver is the center of consciousness and the seat of passions. By ordering the eagle to eat my liver, Zeus is not only causing me pain, he's also depriving me of the spark of mindfulness that makes me what I am. It's a clever way of unnerve me."

"And that is why you didn't want me to see you after noon?"

"There's really nothing to see." Prometheus shrugged. "Without my liver, I'm little more than a husk. Not a charming sight to behold, trust me. Why are you looking at me like that?"

"I've made a decision," I said. "I won't leave this place until you are freed."

Prometheus snorted. "Then I hope you have no one waiting for you where you come from."

"This isn't a jest," I said with emphasis. "I'm serious. I will see you freed, or I will die trying."

"I appreciate your resolution, Zid. It's endearing, really. But I can't expect you to fetch the moon and give it to me, even if you swore it on everything you hold dear."

"So you don't think I can free you?"

"No one but Zeus can."

I nodded toward the chains. "Have you ever tried to break them?"

Prometheus' smile was stretched when he answered. "Break the chain? No, Zid. The god of metalworking Hephaestus made them. I doubt anything could break them except the God of Forges himself, or Zeus."

"We'll see." I approached the chains. I looked around and found a rock as big as my head. I lifted it with effort and hit the chain with all my strength. The rock exploded in a hundred tiny fragments as soon as it touched the metal.

I fell on my back, groaning.

"I told you," Prometheus said. "But thanks for trying."

I stood up, dusting off my vest. "I will help you," I repeated stubbornly. "I will."

"Do you want to help me? Then sit down and play with me."

I started pacing, thinking of what to do.

"Zid?"

"I'm thinking!"

"A game or two might get your mind going."

I looked at the game board. "I'd rather do something *useful* to help you."

"Playing is useful," Prometheus said seriously. "It keeps my mind off the eagle."

I looked at the Titan's face. He was right. At least that I could do to ease his pain. I walked toward the game board and sat cross-legged in front of Prometheus.

We played in silence for a while, both of us wrapped in our own thoughts. My mind was only vaguely aware of what was happening in the game, but by then I had played it enough times to know the rules well. My movements were swift, and I better understood Prometheus's strategy.

I lost two games, but the next one, something else happened.

"You're getting better at this," the Titan said brightly. "You learn fast. It's fun to play with you now."

I could feel the giant's eyes on me. My hands moved swiftly on the game board, my mind now concentrated on the next move.

This time, I realized much earlier, compared with the other games, that I could not win. But maybe I could attempt something else.

"A daring move," Prometheus commented, arching his

eyebrow as he considered his next action. "But it won't bring you far."

He made his move, and I smiled. I moved the last piece, and I looked at the game board with wonder.

"It's a draw," Prometheus said. He looked pleased. "The very first time you managed that. I guess we both lose. Well played." He cleared the board of the remaining pieces. "Now that I think of it, there is something else you can do for me, Zid."

"What is it?"

"You can tell me your stories."

I looked at him, confusion all over my face. "My stories?"

Prometheus started resetting the board. "Long have I spoken," he said, "and yet you have never shared stories of your own. You are a traveler, Zid. I'm sure there is something entertaining you can tell me that will help me keep my mind off my burden."

"Um ... Well, yes," I said, reluctantly. "I can tell stories, but you have seen the making of the world. I mean, I doubt anything could match *that*."

"Maybe I don't want a breathtaking story," Prometheus said, shaking his head. "Have you ever thought about that? Maybe, after so many years chained to this rock, I would be content to hear what kind of food folk in your homeland eat when celebrating a wedding. Maybe I want to know what flowers grow in the land of the Crescent Moon, and if women still make a draught of spice and powdered plants to win the love of young men. Simple things, you see? Can you do that, Zid? Can you tell me a story that has no gods or monsters in it?"

For the very first time since I met Prometheus, I looked at him and didn't see a giant. All I saw was a prisoner. I studied the deep lines beneath his eyes, his slouched shoulders, the way he brushed his fingers on his abdomen, as if to make sure his liver was still there. I saw *somebody*, rather than a deity, a poor being who had been tortured for generations, someone who had to suffer pain and solitude in silence. He was broken, a god brought to the edge of desperation, who fought madness with a simple game of stones.

"Yes," I said after a long while, smiling at him. "I can do that."

I started talking. At first, the words felt awkward and stumbling. But the more I talked, the more I gained confidence, for I was always the one person who spoke around a fire if there were ears ready to listen.

I told Prometheus the three ways a Samarhin nun can play the unthori flute: one to catch the birds, one to make people sleep, and one to chase any worries away. I told him about the gift of gold and silver that lovers in Egypt exchange before the wedding, to seal their promise of love. I told him about the way the druids in the forest of Jassan help pregnant women by giving them magic herbs they harvest in the deepest part of the wood, singing power inside them. I told him how the dark-skinned nomads in the Red Land guard their water as if it were a treasure chest full of gemstones. I told him some of the simple things I knew, and watched his reaction.

Prometheus listened with his eyes closed, as if he was *seeing* my stories, bringing them to life with his imagination. When he opened his eyes again, the tension had left him.

"You are a wonderful storyteller, Zid," he said. "I could peer into a world that has been hidden from me in my seclusion. You see? You didn't have to break those chains. You freed me, if for a brief moment. It's more than anyone has ever done. Please tell me more. Tell me about your family."

I nodded, no longer afraid my words would be meaningless. "As you wish."

I told him about the day my parents exchanged their promise of forever in secret, since neither of their parents wanted them to marry. I told him how they ran away and found love anywhere they wished.

I told him of all the courts, cities and backwater villages where we lived, how my father's traveling inspired me to explore the world. I told him how my mother taught me how to sing and to be brave. I told him how she died, taken by a fever that consumed her slowly, how she fought the illness until there was nothing left of her but void emptiness. I told him how I buried my father with not a tear in my eyes, for he lived the life he wanted to live.

Prometheus listened in silence, nodding now and then, taking in every word with a grateful smile.

"Now tell me about your family," I said to him when my tale was over.

"My family?" The Titan's smile faded. "I'm afraid there is less fondness in the memory of my blood."

"No one's family is perfect," I said.

"I guess that is a way to put it." Prometheus exhaled slowly. "Very well. My family. Where to begin?"

Prometheus spoke about his stern father Iapetus, the Titan called Piercer, who held Uranus firmly in place while his brother Cronus castrated him with a sickle. He told me about the nymph Asia, his mother, who had never cared for any of her children. He said the one thing she excelled in was scheming against her thousands of sisters, to get favors in the court of her father, Oceanus.

Prometheus also seemed to have little love for his brothers.

"Atlas was warlike and arrogant," he said, "and as stern as my father. He was among the Titans who fought the hardest against Zeus. My other brother, Menoetius, was haughty and full of hatred, and twice as violent as Atlas. My only fond memories rest with my younger brother Epimetheus." Prometheus's lips curled into a smile at the name, as if the very sound made him happy. "We were close and cared for each other. As you saw from my memories, he sided with the Olympians when the Titan War began. I loved him very much. He had a genuine talent for shapeshifting and always made me laugh when he turned into the strangest sort of creature, like a monkey with a goat's head, or a donkey with octopus legs. Atlas and Menoetius called him halfwitted, my father thought him a fool, and my mother disregarded him as a failure. He might not have had the brightest mind, but he was kind, and his heart was true. When he was entrusted to distribute the gifts to all the creatures, he forgot to give a gift to the humans. He was very sorry and ashamed. He came to me for help. Epimetheus genuinely wanted to help you mortals but didn't know how."

"And that is why you stole the sacred fire?"

Prometheus lowered and raised his head briefly.

"What happened to him?"

"He disappeared," Prometheus said. "Some said he drank dystheos, the same poison Zeus had given to Cronus and the other Titans who opposed him, and found a way to kill himself. They said he did it for shame over his many failures, one of which was to marry Pandora and to allow her to release sickness, death and many more evils into the world." The Titan looked toward the west, eyes staring at nothing. "I miss his good-hearted foolishness. He was the only Titan with a heart I ever knew."

We kept talking until the sun crept its way up the sky.

It was the moment I had been waiting for.

I stood, dusted off my vest and said farewell. This was the first time I was eager to leave.

I had an eagle to kill.

8

ARROWS OF DESTINY

I waited for the eagle to come, peeking from a safe spot midway between where Prometheus was standing and the base of the mountain. From there, I could see the entire platform.

I heard the high-pitched shriek, and then the shadow fell from the sky. She was as big and as terrible as I remembered, and for a few heartbeats, all I could do was to gasp at the monster. Then I remembered why I was there. As the eagle moved to attack Prometheus, I grasped the red-painted arrow between the thumb and index finger of my right hand, my left hand holding the bow parallel to the ground, waist-high. I nocked the poisonous arrow and then aimed at the bird's body.

The arrow whipped the air, hissing like a snake with demoniac speed, and then ... it bounced off the eagle's chest.

I watched, stunned, as the arrow spiraled down and disappeared at the base of the mountain. I must have hit a rock nearby, I thought, missing the monster by a few inches.

The beast bellowed. Her entire body arched back, her eyes went wide.

I quickly nocked another arrow and shot. This time I was sure the arrow would hit her ... and it did, but it bounced off her with a metallic *clang*.

"Impossible." I stared at her reddish-brown plumage. I realized it shone dully under the sun, and then it dawned on me: It didn't *look* like bronze. It *was* bronze.

The bird snapped her head, her eyes looking toward my direction. I pressed myself against the side of the mountain to hide, but it was too late. She'd seen me.

The monstrous creature flapped her gigantic wings and a gust of wind hit me, so strong it knocked the air out of me. The bow dropped from my hand, bounced on the ground and fell off the mountain.

Again the eagle flapped her wings, causing me to hit my head hard on the wall. I lost my balance and thrashed, desperately trying to grab something as the eagle's wind kept pushing me off my precarious hiding spot. The world became a spinning blur of shapes as I tried to find something to hold on to. Finally, I found a ledge and grasped it with all my strength.

I shook my head to clear it and looked up. The eagle's nostrils flared, her eyes fixed on me. She flexed her legs and was about to take off to finish me.

I heard a cry that echoed throughout the valley, and then I saw Prometheus throwing himself against the winged monster. The Titan delivered a mighty punch to the bird's neck, and the beast backed away, shrieking.

Prometheus stumbled forward. He peeked over the cliff, a bloody hand over his stomach. "Go!" he said. "Now!"

The Titan turned and seized one of the bird's wings, pulling it toward him. His muscles were tensed in the effort to hold the eagle. I could see the chains restraining his movements.

I barely pulled myself up. "Prometheus," I whispered. My head was heavy. I tasted blood in my mouth. I looked up and saw the Titan covered in white blood. The eagle had freed herself from the giant's grip and had sent him crashing to the ground with her full weight.

"No," I wailed. "Prometheus!"

This time, the eagle did not stop at the liver. She was furious. She attacked the Titan's head and broke the left part of his skull with her sharp beak. A burst of pearl blood poured from the giant's head. The monster went on, tearing apart the skin on his chest and shoulders.

After what felt like a thousand years, the bloodbath stopped. The eagle glanced around but seemed to have forgotten me. She flexed her legs and flew away. The peak was silent.

My vision was blurry. I had strained every muscle of my body in the effort to keep myself from falling. I didn't care. I hauled myself up until I reached the platform.

When I saw the Titan sprawled on the ground, the breath was smashed from my chest. His entire body had been torn apart. There was so much blood that, as I walked toward Prometheus, my boots were drenched in it.

I started when I realized his eyes were open, his breathing a slow, rasping sound.

"Prometheus?" I called, falling on my knees right beside him. "Can you hear me?"

The Titan didn't answer. His eyes were open, but they had lost all their brightness. They looked like the cooling embers of a hearth left to extinguish. He kept staring forward, like a lifeless puppet, unaware of my presence.

"Please, son of Iapetus. Answer me." I moved his head gently, so that his eyes could see me.

A string of saliva drooled from his mouth.

Suddenly, his words came back to me.

For us Titans, the liver is the center of consciousness and the seat of passions. By ordering the eagle to eat my liver, Zeus is not only causing me pain, he's also depriving me of the spark of mindfulness that makes me what I am.

I swallowed. Of course. Prometheus's spark of life, his ingenuity, curiosity and bright mind, it was all gone. I finally understood why Prometheus didn't want me to see him like that. He was right: I was staring at nothing but an empty husk, so far away from the kind and lively giant I knew.

That was Zeus's real punishment. No doubt, for the Olympian god that cruelty must have been poetic justice. As Prometheus had given us consciousness with the fire, now Zeus was taking away that very thing from him as a reminder of his crime.

"I'm so sorry," I mumbled, tears in my eyes. "So sorry." I took a blanket from my travel sack and put it over him. Then I held on to his hand as long as I could, before exhaustion forced me to sleep.

9

A MEASURE OF WISDOM

When I woke up, the night was slowly giving way to the morning. I was painfully aware of my head pounding, but except for the headache and a few scratches on my arms, I was fine.

Prometheus still sat on the same spot, but his eyes seemed to have regained their familiar shine. I studied his body; his abdomen and chest were still torn, but all the wounds had stopped bleeding and most of his cuts had healed.

"Prometheus," I said hesitantly, fearing he might be still in a vegetative state. "Are you—"

"I wish you hadn't done something so foolish." The giant's words cut through me like a blade made of ice. After the night spent looking at his lifeless stare, I wasn't prepared to face the unnerving edge of his eyes.

"I'm sorry," I said, looking away. "You've every right to be mad at me, but I was trying to help and—"

"And look what came of it."

I closed my mouth. I could think of nothing to atone for my stupidity. I had been so sure I could slay the eagle and win Prometheus's freedom, and all I gained him was more pain.

Prometheus tossed a rock on the ground. It was a piece we used for the Loser's Game. I saw it rolling over the cliff and disappearing from view.

I glanced at the game board and was surprised to find it shattered. It must have happened during the battle between the Titan and the eagle.

The silence stretched between us to the point of becoming uncomfortable. When it became almost unbearable, I made to say something, but Prometheus was faster.

"I forbid you to come back," he said, his voice flat, devoid of any emotion. "I no longer wish to see you."

"I'm sorry for what I did." My reply came out quickly, and it sounded like a plea. "But I made a promise to you. I—"

"You heard what I said. You are not to return. If you do, I will bring my wrath upon you."

"Please listen." I put both hands over my chest. "I didn't mean to—"

"Mortal." Prometheus pushed himself up with effort, his eyes the blinding red of rage. "I've been friendly with you, but you have no idea what I'm capable of, even chained to this rock."

I opened my mouth, but nothing came out of it.

"As I have restored your health, so I can unravel it." Prometheus' voice was low and dangerous now. He pointed toward my leg. "I just need to say a few words, and your body will start crumbling. Do you understand what I'm saying? You will not visit me again. Say it."

I looked into his eyes. "No," I said, surprised at how steady my voice sounded.

Prometheus stared at me. "I won't ask again."

"You have every reason to be mad at me," I said, my pulse drumming in my ears. "If I must die to make amends, so be it." I projected my arms outward. "Do what you wish, Bringer of Fire. I stand on my word. I will see you freed, or I will die trying."

I kept my eyes closed and braced myself for a blow. I waited for something, anything, to happen, but the only thing that hit me was the icy wind scourging the mountain.

I heard Prometheus sigh. I opened my eyes just in time to see the Titan sinking down on the ground, groaning. He rested his head back against the rock, one hand over his stomach.

"You are as stubborn as a bull, Zid." He tossed a look at my travel sack. "Do you have anything stronger than water in there?"

I looked at my bag, confused. "I have spiced wine," I said slowly.

"That will do."

I passed him the wine, and he took a long swallow. "This is good," he said, eying the wineskin.

"Really?" I frowned. "That's cheap vintage that people from the village buy from nomads who know more of milk than grapes."

Prometheus chuckled at my joke. He tipped the wineskin back and swallowed twice before returning the wine. "What can I say? I'm happy with little things."

I wet my throat with the thick, bitter liquid, then held it out with a little shake.

We traded the wineskin in silence, the wine somehow tasting a little better every time the Titan handed it back to me.

"So." I cleared my throat, dusted my vest. "You're no longer angry at me?"

"It's hard to be mad at the only friend I have."

That struck me in a way I couldn't have fathomed. The word *friend*, spoken so lightly, made me smile.

"Will you be fine?" I looked at his wounds.

Prometheus waved a hand dismissively. "They will be gone in less than an hour."

"The eagle," I said, thinking of the moment I nearly died. "My arrows bounced off her. I think her plumage is made out of bronze."

Prometheus nodded. "One of Hephaestus' finest works. The maker of my chains has been entrusted by Zeus to create an armor to protect my torturer. Killing that eagle is almost impossible." He studied the ground a few feet away from him, grimacing. "She has shattered the game board and blown away most of the pieces. They will be halfway down the valley by now."

"Don't worry," I said. "We can make a new game board."

Prometheus barked a laugh. "You're quite the optimist, aren't you?"

I shrugged. "If you start your journey focusing on the bad things, you'll see only bad things."

"Is that traveler's wisdom?"

"Just something my father used to say."

Prometheus leaned in closer to me. "Why do you want to help me so badly, Zid? Is it just thankfulness?"

"No," I said, realizing my will to see the Titan free was stronger than ever. "It's much more than that. I want you to see the cities I described in my stories: Babylon and Troy and all the other jewels in the west. I want you to meet the people I told you about, to breathe and feel the cultures that nurture them. I want you to be there, to see the wonders humankind has created since the dawn of civilization. Perhaps I can't break those chains and I can't kill the eagle, but there must be a way to win your freedom."

The Titan rubbed at his forearms, his eyes resting on his chains. "Freedom is not an option, Zid."

"Why not?"

Prometheus threw another rock over the cliff. "There's something I left out when I told you about my story. Zeus chained me as a punishment for stealing the fire, but the eagle was not part of the punishment in the beginning."

"What do you mean?"

"He's sending the eagle because I hold a secret that will destroy him."

Again the word *secret*. Prometheus tossed it like a dagger in the midst of a map, signaling a direction. "What secret?" I asked.

"A prophecy I hold close to my chest," Prometheus said. He looked around once again, as if making sure of something. "I'm not called Forethought without a reason."

I finally understood why sometimes he paused and looked westward before talking of the gods. He was making sure they weren't listening.

The Titan threw yet another rock over the cliff. I heard it tumble until the sound was swallowed in silence. "This I know." Prometheus clasped his hands into fists and stared at the sky. "Zeus is bound to be killed by the offspring he'll have with the Nereid Thetis. The Fates do have a peculiar sense of humor, don't you think? Zeus is destined to be overthrown by his own son. The same destiny his father Cronus suffered."

I swallowed. The magnitude of what the giant had said made my head spin. "Does Zeus know this prophecy exists?"

"He knows someone will threaten him, yes." Prometheus

turned his head and looked at me. "He has sent many times the messenger god Hermes to convince me to reveal the prophecy. I have always refused, even when he offered to lighten my sentence, even when he offered to stop sending the eagle."

"Why are you going through the pain if you can at least avoid *that*?"

"Because vengeance is a plate best served cold." Prometheus' words had a sharpness to them that didn't seem to belong to the Titan. "If I keep the secret, and Zeus falls, I will free humanity from its greatest tyrant. Don't you see, Zid? Gods are petty and vengeful. Without the King of Gods to hold the Olympians, they might war against each other, trying to seize his power. And in doing so, humanity will be free of the gods for the first time in history. Do you understand now, my friend? The pain I endure, I endure it for you. I do this for humankind."

Prometheus' hands were shaking. When he looked at me again, his eyes were like torches. "I know how my story ends. This mountain is my prison and my grave. This is my destiny. I accept it." He took another swig from the canteen. "I really like this vintage," he said, his eyes far away. "Please, bring more."

He gave back the canteen. I stared at it, thinking of what he had said.

"I'm so tired." Prometheus's eyebrows pulled together, the frown deep and evident. "I think I will sleep now." He rested his head on the rock and closed his eyes.

I let him sleep, watching him for a long time as his massive chest rose and fell. My eyes lingered on the blanket I gave him the night before. It was soaked with his blood. I stood on the platform quietly so as not to disturb his rest and picked up one of the square-shaped pieces of the Loser's Game.

As I looked at it, it suddenly occurred to me that both Prometheus and Zeus were trying to win a game; Prometheus by holding his secret until Zeus's fall, Zeus by keeping him bound, torturing the Titan until he gave up. And in doing so, they had been dragged toward a draw in which both were destined to lose.

I glanced at Prometheus one last time before heading back to the village.

I realized then what my role was. I needed to be the needle that tipped the scale.

And I knew exactly how to do it.

10

THE WILL THAT BROKE THE SKY

The valley between the mountains and the village looked hollow. No birds chirping, not even insects buzzing; there was nothing but a few dry trees wasting away under the sun. Everything was as bare as death.

It was the best spot for a stand against the gods.

I looked at my hand, closed into a fist, and felt the sharp object inside. I had no idea if my plan would work, but it was the best one I had.

Once, my father told me that the best way to make a decision was to imagine my life without the freedom to choose. How would that life look? What would be the thing you missed the most?

I had imagined myself walking away from my promise to Prometheus, leaving the Titan to his fate.

No matter how hard I tried, I could not bear the thought of abandoning him.

And so I decided to challenge fate itself, regardless of its cost. I was going to speak with the only god with the power to free Prometheus, and I wasn't going to accept no for an answer.

I looked at the sky, toward the west, toward Olympus.

"God of Thunder!" I called out, a cold shiver running through my bones as I spoke the words. "My name is Zid, son of Xhoroast. Long you have sought the prophecy of your downfall. Long it has eluded you. No more. I'm here to offer you a bargain. I know what

Prometheus knows. I'm willing to reveal it to you, Storm-Bringer, if you will come."

The sky remained an even sheet of bright blue, occasionally dotted by small clouds. The chill wind rustling through the branches of the skeleton trees was the only answer the gods sent me.

"Lord of Olympus!" I called with renewed strength. "Please. Let this be—"

"You're wasting your breath, mortal."

I spun. Behind me, somebody was leaning on one of the bare plants, hands behind his head. He was of average height, not much taller than me, but leaner, the line of his body straight as an arrow. His skin was light pink, almost pale, his eyes as black as jet stone. He was wearing a golden vest and golden sandals. They had wings attached to them.

Prometheus had spoken to me of the Olympians enough that I could easily recognize their messenger.

"Hermes." I bowed my head to acknowledge him. "You grace me with your presence, although I was expecting someone else."

"The Immortal Sky Father is not a god to be summoned." Hermes raised his eyebrows and gave me a glassy stare. "He sends me. What is it that you wish to say to the King of Kings?"

"I'd rather speak with Zeus himself, Herald of the Gods."

Hermes scoffed. "I'd rather spend my time staring at naked nymphs than standing amid this rocky desolation." The god glanced around as if the very air of that place stained him. "You see? We're both bound to disappointment. Say what you need to say."

"I have something to offer to Zeus."

"Yes, mortal, I have ears. I heard you yelling at the sky." Hermes rubbed his forehead with a thumb. "What a dull way to spend my morning. You claim to know the Titan's prophecy."

"It's not a claim," I said firmly. "I heard it from Prometheus himself."

"What makes you think he spoke the truth?"

"He's my friend," I said. "He has no reason to lie."

"Friend?" Hermes cocked his head then shook it. "You think

the Titan is your *friend*? He must have gone mad if he treats you as such."

"Considering what Prometheus has told me about you Olympians, I don't expect you to understand a concept like friendship."

Hermes stepped up to me. "You do realize I can squeeze the truth off you as easily as an elephant squashing a melon?" His black eyes bored into mine. "I'm not fond of torture, but we do what we must to go about our day."

That made me smile. Prometheus's stories were accurate indeed. These gods were predictable.

"I doubt you could squash the truth out of a dead man." I opened my hand and showed the contents to Hermes. "This arrowhead has been dipped into purplehead snake poison. If it so much as pierces my skin, it'll kill me in a few heartbeats. All I need to do is squeeze and Zeus's only chance to survive the prophecy will be gone forever."

Hermes' stretched smile didn't touch his eyes. "You wouldn't dare."

"I saw what Zeus did to my friend," I said. I slowly closed my hand around the arrowhead. "I won't live another day and let that happen again."

Hermes glanced at my closing fist, said nothing.

"You will meet my condition, Olympian," I said, "or Zeus will fall."

Hermes narrowed his eyes at me. "Are you threatening the King of all Gods, mortal?"

"I don't need to. Fate itself is doing the job for me."

The messenger of the gods studied me carefully. "You would really die for the Titan?"

"I would."

The Olympians' eyes flashed with a mischievous light. "Ah!" he clapped his hands. "That's entertaining! You're fun, little man. This subterfuge makes you worthy of my attention. Let's hear it, then. What is that you want in exchange for the prophecy?"

"I want Prometheus unbound. I want Zeus to swear on the sacred River Styx he will set him free."

Hermes' eyes widened. He knew what I was asking. Among the many stories Prometheus had told me, he hadn't neglected the one about the goddess of the river Styx. During the Titan war, Styx sided with the Olympians, as Prometheus and Epimetheus did. After the war, Zeus declared that every oath sworn upon the river that bore her name would be binding. Not even Zeus could break such an oath.

"Madness," Hermes said between clenched teeth. "You dare call me here to mock the gods? To squander our time on jests and nothing?"

"It's not a jest. It's my only condition."

Hermes snorted. "Aren't you aware why the all-father keeps him chained?"

"I know he doesn't trust him. I know he thinks he might do something else to overthrow him."

"Then you know why he cannot be freed. He's a Titan and a trickster. His very nature can't be trusted."

"What if he no longer were a Titan? What if he was to be stripped of all his powers, as happened to Cronus and all the other Titans who opposed Zeus?"

The Herald of the Gods gave me a blank look. "What are you trying to say?"

I showed Hermes my canteen. "What if I gave him a draught of dystheos, without him realizing it? What if he was to bleed out his divinity? Would Zeus still think of him as a threat?"

Hermes' smile showed his perfect teeth as he studied me with renewed interest. "You want to trick the trickster?"

"I told you. I'm his friend. He trusts me."

The god burst out in throaty laughter. "I was wrong about you, mortal. There's more than meets the eye in your dull look." He glanced to the sky and nodded. "Yes. Maybe we can reach an agreement after all."

∿

THE NEXT DAY I went to visit Prometheus, my canteen filled with spiced wine mixed with a fine powder as black as night.

Handing the cursed draught to Prometheus was one of the hardest things I had ever done, but I did it.

The Titan drank eagerly, suspecting nothing. I felt so bad I wanted to throw up, but I stayed with him, and conversed until noon came and I said my farewells.

As I was walking away, my heart filled with an odd mix of fulfillment and guilt, and no screams came from the mountain.

When I arrived at the village, the people looked at me strangely. They stepped away from my path and whispered as I walked by. One of them caught my eyes. It was the elder of the village who rented me his hut.

"The mountain is quiet for the first time in generations," he said, his eyes searching mine. "What have you done to the demon?"

I glanced over my shoulder. "I've bribed the gods," I said, a sour taste in my mouth. "I bought his freedom."

"How?"

"By destroying a friendship," I said. The words felt like a piece of burning coal tearing its way through wool. "I'll leave tomorrow. Thanks for your hospitality."

I couldn't sleep that night, so I went out under the starry sky and looked at the peaks, thoughts swirling in my head. I felt dirty, unworthy of the air I was breathing. If there were any justice in the world, I thought at that moment, I'd drop dead any minute now.

But I didn't die. I kept breathing.

Justice is an ethereal concept, prone to be bent by any will. It was Zeus's idea of justice that resulted in Prometheus's imprisonment and torture. My own idea of justice came with a hefty price: in order to free my friend, I had to betray him.

I thought of the first day I arrived in the village, eager to know the truth behind the story. It felt like a thousand years had passed. It felt like it had happened to another person.

I stood there, letting the cold wind bite its sharp teeth into my skin, until the sun rose and the light banished all shadows. At that point, only the seeker remained.

I took my travel sack and set out to go to the mountain.

I might have been a traitor, but I wasn't going to leave my friend guessing what had happened.

I was going to tell him to his face.

After all he did for me, I owed him the truth.

~

WHEN I REACHED THE PLATFORM, for a moment I thought it was empty. Then, my eyes met a figure staring at a set of broken chains. It took me a while to recognize him.

"Prometheus?" I said, a wave of fear coursing through my body.

The Titan lifted his head. He had lost nearly all his distinctive features. He was no longer fifteen feet tall, for a start. Now he was just a few inches taller than me. His skin had turned pink; his blazing eyes were now emerald green. He looked like a human being.

"It was in the wine, wasn't it?" he said, his hands folded in his lap. "The dystheos." His voice was the only thing that remained the same: a rolling, baritone sound that carried itself like an avalanche.

"Yes," I said. "Yes, it was."

A grim smile twisted the Titan's mouth. "How did you get it?"

I pressed my lips, swallowed. It took all my courage to look him in the eyes. "I bargained with the Olympians. Your freedom in exchange for the prophecy."

"Hmm." Prometheus straightened up, looking small and fragile. "You taught me a new thing today, Zid," he said with a dry smile. "Friendship can be a double-edged sword. Do you understand what you have done? With Zeus gone, humankind would have been freed of his tyranny."

"And you would have been stuck here for eternity, going mad."

"It was a sacrifice I was willing to make."

"What worth is freedom if one doesn't have a friend to share it with in the journey of life?"

Prometheus contemplated his broken chains, then he looked back at me. "Another bit of traveler's wisdom?"

I shook my head. I reached into my travel sack and took out my mother's statuette. "Just something my mother used to say."

The Titan studied my father's work. "I would have liked to meet her. Your father, too. They sound like interesting people."

I took a step in Prometheus's direction. "I came here because I betrayed you." The words tasted like poison as I spoke them. I was very aware of the empty feeling in the pit of my stomach, but I didn't care. My mouth was as dry as sand, but I kept talking. "I know I don't deserve your forgiveness, but I genuinely think that killing Zeus wasn't the best gift you could give to humankind."

Prometheus regarded me with his new, strikingly green eyes. "If not that, then what?"

I clasped my hands around the statuette. "Staying alive and seeing how far humankind has gone since Zeus chained you."

Prometheus seemed to consider my words, his eyebrows close together. "Seeing how far humankind has gone?"

"Think about it," I said, pulling in a deep breath. "Now that Zeus doesn't see you as a threat to his dominion, you are free to inspire humankind as you did at the beginning of civilization. There are men and women out there ready to welcome that gift. I saw many of these inquisitive minds in my travels. My father was one of them. I think, now that you are free, there is no limit to the wonders we can achieve."

"I understand why you did it," Prometheus said, nodding slowly. "I truly do, but I'm afraid I will never be able to justify your action. You lost much more than you can imagine by letting him live."

I put my mother's statuette in his palm and closed his hand around it. "It's a sacrifice I'm willing to make."

The Titan stared at me, a dazed look on his face. "Zid—"

"I know I don't deserve your friendship," I said, "but please, accept this gift. It's yours."

Prometheus looked at the statuette, his fingers tracing the fine lines of my mother's face.

I turned, took my bag and walked away.

"Wait."

I stopped in mid-stride, my bag bouncing on my back. I felt a human-size hand on my shoulder. "You didn't betray me, Zid," Prometheus said. "I'm afraid you're wrong about that, too. You acted like a friend, something I never had."

I turned and regarded the Titan. He was looking at the rocky ground where he lay the night the eagle ravaged him, extinguishing his consciousness. "I forgot what it was like to move without a chain, without having to fear the rising of the sun. I forgot what it was like to breathe as a free being. And now I remember." He squeezed my shoulder gently and smiled at me. "Thanks to you."

I stared at those green eyes, wise and welcoming, letting the rustling of rocks on the ground fill in the silence, fighting back tears. Then, I took the first carefree breath in a long time. I smiled back, offered my hand, and Prometheus shook it.

"I could use a friend to walk my way down from this prison," Prometheus said, looking down the mountain. "This new body feels like a loosened vest. I'll need time to get used to it."

We made our descent slowly. Sometimes Prometheus paused and looked back, as if expecting something to keep him from moving. Maybe he was feeling the ghost of the chains that no longer bound him to the rock. Maybe he thought he was dreaming and was afraid he would wake up.

"You're not going back there," I reassured him, stressing each word. "From now on, we're just moving forward."

Prometheus nodded. "Thank you," he said. At that moment, a heavy burden seemed to have been eased off his shoulders and his whole posture relaxed.

When we reached the base of the mountain, the Titan looked stunned. He touched the dark-gray rocky wall, whispered a few words I couldn't grasp, and then he followed me. We made the rest of the way in silence, and when we arrived at the village, everyone around stopped and looked in our direction. They stared at Prometheus, their eyes lingering on the two deep lines of red on his wrists, where his chains had been. They looked at one another as if to make sure they were all seeing the stranger.

"They are all so different," the Titan said to me, taking tentative steps toward the forming crowd. "So far from the first of humankind I created. They are shorter, their faces narrower. There are so many details I didn't put in. And there are so many of them. Are we in a big city?"

I laughed at his ecstatic expression. "A big city? This is a small backwater village so tiny it has no place on a map. If this village looks big to you, wait till you see Byblos, Troy and Babylon. You might be in for one wild surprise."

Prometheus was about to reply when his eyes caught something. I followed his stare. A dozen yards away, the blacksmith of the village was hard at work in his workshop, unaware of the outside clamor. Prometheus walked in that direction, the crowd moving away to let him pass.

"Prometheus?" I called him. "Where are you going?"

He kept going without even glancing at me. I called him again, and again he ignored me. Muttering under my breath, I trailed after him.

The blacksmith, a short, middle-aged man with arms bigger than my legs, lifted his gaze when Prometheus stopped in front of him.

"Greetings," the Titan said as I caught up to him.

The stocky man looked at me, then at Prometheus. He stroked his thick, charcoal-black beard and lifted his bushy eyebrows. "What can I do for ya?"

"That's a fine tool you're making." Prometheus nodded toward the blacksmith's work. "Is that a chisel?"

"Aye." The blacksmith lifted the tool, still ember-colored with the memory of the fire. "Be ready before the sun kneels, stranger." He eyed the Titan and cleared his throat. "Care to buy it?"

Prometheus glanced behind the blacksmith, to a far corner of the workshop where the furnace was harboring a lively fire. "Perhaps another time," he said. "I'm just glad you find it useful."

"What?" The blacksmith glanced at the chisel, frowning. He raised the soon-to-be-made tool and said, "This?"

"No." Prometheus glanced at the furnace. "The fire. It cost dearly to bring it to you. I'm happy to see you're putting it to good use."

The blacksmith turned to regard the fire as though he was missing something important, then looked at the Titan, his eyes bulging.

I entered the blacksmith's workshop and put a hand on Prometheus's shoulder. "Are you ready?" I asked.

Prometheus's green eyes lightened, and he smiled. "I'm ready," he said. "Show me the way."

EPILOGUE

I n the middle of nowhere, halfway between the village and the valley, we found the small girl with dirty-blond hair. She was holding the reins of three saddled horses, waiting for us.

I blinked, glanced back at the village now far behind us, then walked up to her. "What are you doing here?" I asked.

But she wasn't looking at me. She was looking at the tall man beside me.

"Long have I awaited this moment," she said, stepping forward. "I was afraid it would never come."

Prometheus studied the girl, then burst out laughing. "I thought he might have been aided by someone," he said, glancing at me. "But I didn't think it was you, Epimetheus."

I looked at the girl, then back at Prometheus. "Epimetheus?" I said, rubbing my eyes. "Your *brother* Epimetheus? I ... I don't understand."

"Look more closely," the girl said, grinning. The wind started rising, and her hair flowed freely. Her legs and arms stretched; her body changed shape, becoming taller and thicker. Her rags became a long, dark, hooded garment, and her face grew a thick, brown beard.

I stepped back, blinking slowly. It was the nomad who first told me the story of the shadow demon.

"You?" I blurted. "Why ... why the disguise?"

"I couldn't reveal myself to you, for the gods were watching." Epimetheus pointed at the sky. "But they never considered a human a threat, so I changed my shape to guide you. I thank you for saving him. I'm in your debt." The Titan looked at Prometheus. "Brother, I have failed you many times and I'm ashamed of that, but I'm standing here today because I found hope. When an oracle told me you could be saved only by your own creation, I set out to find someone like Zid: a curious mind with a true heart."

"Someone like me?" I said with an incredulous stare. "What ... what do you mean?"

Epimetheus placed both hands on my shoulders. "I know you, Zid, son of Xhoroast. It wasn't an easy task to find a man like you, a man meant to challenge the gods and to end an injustice as old as humankind."

I looked into the Titan's eyes, which were bright and filled with something I could only describe as awe.

"I was there when you were little more than six," Epimetheus said, closing his eyes, pulling in a deep breath, "when you decided to climb a tree just to prove to yourself you could. I was there when you waited the night out, discovering the dawn for the first time. I was there when Archena, the girl you fell in love with, died because of fear, and you swore to yourself you would never let something like that happen again. I was there when a lion wounded your leg." He opened his eyes again and smiled a thin smile. "I was there to make sure you didn't lose it. I'm just sorry I couldn't do more than patch your wound as best I could. I've never had my brother's gift for healing."

My whole body went still. "You ... you mean ..." I stammered, my mouth falling open. "You're saying ... you were there? You were the healer?"

"Yes, Zid. I've been beside you all of those times." The Titan peeked at his brother, and then his eyes went back to me. "I saw you stumbling more times than I can count, I saw you falling. Each time, you picked yourself up and continued your journey until it brought you here." Epimetheus nodded, as though suddenly struck by a realization. "You're more similar to my brother than I'll ever be. There is the same fire of defiance inside you, the same drive to explore further, to become more than what you are. You've lost things in the past, but you've also gained so much. You're not afraid to challenge yourself, you're not scared to sacrifice what you are for the promise of what you might become."

Epimetheus walked past me and kneeled in front of Prometheus, his eyes downcast. "Brother, my failures are undeniable, forged into the history of the world, impossible to ignore. But if you'll forgive me, I pledge I'll follow you and atone for my sins by helping humankind be free from the oppression of the gods."

Prometheus pulled his brother up and embraced him. "There is nothing to forgive," he said, his eyes shiny with the promise of tears. "We are united again. It's all that matters."

I watched those two brothers together, after how long apart only the gods knew. At that moment I realized everything I did for Prometheus had been worth it, just to be able to see that embrace.

Prometheus released his younger brother, and Epimetheus handed us the reins. We mounted the horses in silence, moving in unison as if following the steps of a well-known path.

"So, seeker," Prometheus asked, smiling at me. "Where shall we go next?"

"Well," I said, smiling back, "I think it's about time the Bringer of Fire sees the light humankind is using to cast away the shadows."

The End

MUSE OF AVALON

BOOK IV

1

SEEKERS OF GLORY

Fools like this man come all the time to my mountain. The promise of glory brings them to me with their chins held up, their heads already polluted with images of bards singing songs about the great deeds they have accomplished, even before they are accomplished. Each, in his mind's eye, sees the royal court filled with people toasting him. And himself, gazing at the crowd, a crown upon his head.

Fools, as I said.

It all starts the same way. Somebody tells him the story I spread long ago, or at least a version of that story. It promises him power as the ruler of a nation. That is why they are here, these aspiring heroes, to pull the sword out of the stone.

So few realize it's not about the glory; it's not about the crown. These are just consequences of the valor they are supposed to already possess. What they need to prove their worth is courage, integrity, and a spirit of self-sacrifice for a bigger cause.

None of them has any idea that I live inside this sword, a goddess who chose to bind her soul to the iron of this blade. How could they know? It's not a part of the story they heard. I left out that part, for a reason.

It pains me to realize that after all this time, after so many men have come and attempted to pull the sword from the stone, I can predict who has a chance and who is doomed to fail from the very beginning.

Always, I hope I am wrong.

Look at this man, standing in front of me.

When he reached the mountaintop, his eyes were eager and his mouth half-opened in a satisfied smile. He thought the hard part was behind him. The mountaintop is flat and wide enough for a dozen men to stand abreast.

He is catching his breath now. Climbing the mountain is a long and hard task, filled with peril. There are poisonous snakes and scorpions lurking between the rocks, and the cliff-like slope is steep and razor-sharp.

Many men abandon the quest after merely looking at the mountain. Others wish they had done so when they are halfway up.

But this one made it here, and I suppose I should give him some credit, and maybe the benefit of the doubt.

He is a tall fellow, his shoulders wide and round as water pots turned upside down. A British lord, by the look of him. He wears a coat made of furs the color of dry maple lumber; his hands are hidden in leather gloves. A lion breathing fire is painted on his breastplate.

I try to imagine the way he must have heard of the sword— from a sailor or a fisherman, perhaps, maybe from a farmer if he'd ventured into the countryside. When his eyes catch the iron of the weapon, they glint with desire.

He moves toward me, glances at the metal scabbard beside me that, too, is thrust inside the stone, with a magic even I cannot undo. His eyes brush past the riddle written in the stone, meant to help the seeker find the only way to draw me out of the mountaintop. He grunts at the riddle, as if it is unimportant. I wonder if he can read. The scabbard he disregards quickly.

Typical.

What he wants is the promise of the legend. He who can draw me from the stone will become the king of a nation. An enticing promise, and all this man cares about.

When he is in front of the sword that is my prison, his smile is so wide I can see the back row of his teeth. He flexes his biceps;

opens and closes his hands with growing excitement. My fear solidifies. Just another man with his brain in his muscles.

But still I try to maintain hope. Maybe I'm wrong in my assumption. Remember? Give him the benefit of the doubt.

His callous hands close roughly around the hilt, and he tries to pull the sword out of the stone. His smile soon fades, like a half-moon covered by a thick bank of clouds. He grunts and grunts with effort, his teeth set so hard I can see the line of his jaw and the thick, serpent-like vein on his temple. He changes position, tries to pull with his back arched, then flexes his massive legs and pulls with those, too.

He tries for several heartbeats; then he curses and kicks the stone. He breathes in sharply, his hands resting on his hips, his eyes bloodshot. He walks up and down, mumbling something that doesn't go past his lips. Then he looks at me, plants his feet on the ground and tries his luck again.

A very poor start. The last fragment of hope I had fades with each weaker pull he attempts, for it doesn't matter how much he pulls, Heracles himself would get old trying to draw me out of the stone.

If there is something I have learned while watching one failed attempt after another, it is that even when it should be clear that brute force will not do the trick, men are too proud to admit it.

Some of their stubbornness borders on stupidity.

Half a dozen of the past seekers snapped muscles and tendons because they pulled too hard, went too far. A couple of them broke bones trying to lift heavy objects, hoping to move me. One even tried to swing a rock at me but lost his balance, toppled to his side and rolled off the cliff.

The vultures dined well that night.

I don't know how long it takes, but eventually the British lord stops trying. I can see blood where his teeth ground against his gums, and sweat makes his forehead glisten like a stone pulled out of a river. In the end, he curses his gods and releases me from his grip.

There is an infinitesimal part of me that still has hope. I hope now he will think, evaluate his options, maybe figure out that the scabbard is important, that it is not just an ornament put there for no reason. But again, I'm bound to be disappointed. The British man tosses me a bloodshot look, and then he spits at me.

Blaming anything but themselves for their failures: this is how men give up. I'm used to this reaction, but it doesn't mean I've ever liked it.

I make the iron of my blade vibrate ever so slightly, and the air carries a message meant for my friends. A low buzz rises from a nearby bush, and the British man's head turns as his eyes widen. A swarm of bees appears in the air, thick as living smoke, and washes over the seeker. The man turns, flailing and squirming, and starts his way down the mountain.

Here's a story you can share with your tavern friends, if you make it to the bottom.

No one laughs at my joke, and when the man disappears from view, silence falls over my domain once again.

If I could sigh, I would.

I should have known better. How many times have I seen men like him, and how many times have my hopes been shattered?

Maybe I have become so desperate I would gladly let the first man with half a brain have me. Maybe these seekers remind me of my foolishness, of the reason I'm here, trapped inside this sword. Yes, I should have known better. All my years of wisdom, all the things I did, the wonders I saw, the people I inspired. What did it bring me?

I used to talk with gods, to inspire genius in mortal minds, to weave change in history itself, and now all I can do is talk to myself like some madwoman.

A fine rain falls from the iron gray sky. What little remained of the sun has almost vanished below the horizon. Darkness will soon follow, and with it more silence. No man has ever tried to climb the mountain in the dark. It would be madness.

I don't mind staying alone. I had my share of disappointments today, and at least I can enjoy the cool touch of the rain caressing me, cleansing me of the dirt and the sweat.

Maybe I am too harsh with the seekers. I want them to succeed. I really do. But after so long, I recognize patterns. I know what to look for when one of them makes it to the mountaintop. I can spot pride from the bearing of their bodies, stubbornness from the light in their eyes.

This land is full of such men, lovers of war and destruction whose eyes never read a work of genius, whose hands never played an instrument, whose mouths were made for guzzling beer, not for reciting classic poems.

The temperature falls. The moon rises and the last trace of sun is banished from the world.

Another day passes, just another coin tossed into the cup of destiny. It adds to the many days I have been here, secluded by a curse I placed upon myself in the hope of doing good.

Maybe I am the fool, after all.

Now the rain pours down heavily, and I bathe in its coolness, let it wash my restless soul.

It is in a moment like this that my memory goes back to my beloved home, where the olive trees stood tall from horizon to horizon, and the sun shone year-round, bathing the majestic temples filled with art with his warmth. My home, the birthplace of literature, philosophy, drama, and democracy. For a while my mind lingers on that forgotten paradise; then I remember the chaos that followed, the temples and statues brought down, the fire eating scrolls and tables filled with the knowledge of millennia. And after that, my mind goes past the pain and the deprivation that followed, past the interminable journey that brought me to this far land, until unavoidably I am reminded of the isle of Avalon, where all of this started.

2

ASHES AND MIST

When Olympus fell and most of our temples were reduced to rubble by the mortals, my mother, Mnemosyne, was one of the last gods to survive among the powerful Titans. Many of her kin were already dead, and my father Zeus himself had disappeared long before the last Olympians, Poseidon and Hera, had been slain. Someone said the king of gods had been killed too, like most of the mighty Olympians. Others said he turned himself into a human to run away from the slaughter, and that he will live in shame until this world goes dry and is swallowed by a star.

The truth is that I don't know what happened to my father, or to all the surviving gods. All I know is that Mnemosyne used her last whiff of power to allow me and my sisters to flee to Albion, a distant land in the north of Europa I knew almost nothing about.

Our mother forbade us to come back to Greece.

"It's too dangerous here," she warned, her words sharp and urgent. "Our Pantheon is shattering, our kin weakened and scattered." Then she took me aside and looked into my eyes as only she could, with a mixture of maternal love and firmness. "Calliope," she said, "I trust you with the life of your sisters. You are the oldest and the mightiest of them, and all of you are the very heart of our culture, the stewards of our memory. Seek refuge in the north. Albion hosts its own gods; maybe some of them will be willing to shelter you. Once you gain safety, remember who you are. You inspire art, justice and wisdom in the minds of mortals. You make them a better version of themselves. May your justice bathe the barbarian lands you shall call home and bring stability and culture along the way."

"I promise I will, Mother." I said my farewell, doing nothing to hide my tears.

After Poseidon's death, the sea was impossible to travel, so we had to make the journey through Europa inland. I led my sisters north, stopping only to rest in wild forests filled with beasts. After three months of travel, at last we boarded the ship that brought us to Albion.

The northern land welcomed us with mist and rain. The clouds seemed embedded in the sky, stifling the sun and stealing its warmth from all living things.

Albion differed from Greece in many ways. The weather was only one of them. Colder and windier, this land looked more vast and more wet. The country itself brewed a different stock of gods and mortals. We learned later on that most people living there called it Britain.

I was as frightened as my sisters, but I could not show it. I was supposed to take care of them. We had been driven from our safe home, and now we needed to survive in this land where everything looked strange.

My mother had suggested that we find allies, bind ourselves with the gods of this land. My sisters and I thought that was sound advice, since we believed our divine origin might help us. We would provide our hosts with our divine knowledge in exchange for refuge in their halls.

We were wrong.

Dangerous gods were worshipped here. Cross-legged gods holding torches and ram-headed snakes with eyes the color of fire. Healing deities who gathered near thermal springs, who slept with lizards and dined on insects. Violent horse goddesses, keepers of battle and slaughter, who coupled with beasts and tore flesh from human bodies with teeth as sharp as knives.

Most of them valued blood, sorcery and dark magic over everything else. Their laws were alien to us, their code of conduct impossible to decipher. They fought constantly among themselves and were not welcoming to us. They seemed to have no unified law that governed their cosmos. Even Zeus himself had to bow before the Fates, but these gods were rogues. They did what they wished, when they wished. After we made a few attempts to befriend them, most ignored us, but a few hunted us.

My sisters Erato and Clio were wounded by a horned god of war, and a club-wielding god drawing along a company of men whose ears were chained to his tongue almost killed poor Thalia.

"It's no use," Clio said, after yet another attack from a native god who tried to enslave us. She ran a hand through her short black hair, shaking her head as she did so. "These gods have no interest in helping us, Calliope. They are bloodthirsty monsters, only interested in destruction and war. We have nothing of value to offer to them."

She was right. My mother had meant well when she counseled us to find allies in this far land, but she had assumed Albion's gods would be alike us.

"We should go back," said a frightened Polyhymnia, her chestnut-brown eyes wide with fear. "We should never have left Greece."

"No," I said. "Our home is burning, sister. There is no going back. We need to find a safe haven."

My sisters gathered around me. "How do you propose we do that?" Erato asked.

"By finding a virgin land devoid of humans and their deities." I looked at my sisters one by one. "Mortals in Greece used to settle in new lands all the time. We can do the same; we can create a new beginning. It will be more difficult, starting from nothing, but it will be worth it."

"I think we should separate, then," Clio said, and a couple of my sisters nodded in her direction. "It would take less time."

"No." I put a hand on Clio's shoulder. "We're stronger together, and we can protect each other. It's the best chance we have to survive."

It was not an easy task to convince my sisters, but in the end they saw sense in my proposal and we started the long, painful process of finding a home away from home.

We were always on the move, always looking over our shoulders, expecting signs of danger. We steered clear of forests, lakes and caves, since that is where most of the demons, fairies and monsters lived, but that didn't spare us from several more encounters. Each took its toll.

Even though we tried to avoid Albion's deities, it seemed more and more of them found us. We soon realized something had changed: now *they* were looking for us.

Word had spread that foreigner goddesses were walking on their land, seeking refuge. A few of the gods who had managed to wound us proclaimed that our blood was magic, that it could increase their powers.

We became prey: weak, outnumbered and ready to fall.

It was a measure of our desperation that we headed toward a small fishing village, following nothing but a rumor.

Erato had heard a story in a nearby town. The inhabitants spoke of an island off the shore of the mainland, untouched by mortals and gods alike. It was uninhabited and ancient, and sailors around the area called it Avalon, 'the isle of apple trees,' because apples grew all there year-round. Few sailors ever went there. They thought the isle was cursed. By what, we never understood.

We further investigated the rumor and found out the island was real, but none of the villagers wanted anything to do with it because of the curse.

It took me a long time to finally convince a sailor to take us to Avalon. I sold him my last possession, a gift my son Orpheus gave me, the magic lyre he used to attempt to rescue his doomed wife Eurydice from the Underworld.

After we secured safe passage, we landed on the island and found no curse, only a wild, abandoned land ready for the taking. For the first time since we reached Albion, we felt hope.

We wasted no time and used our powers to bless this newfound land. My sister Clio had been a friend of the god Pan, who had taught her how to shape the earth and whisper to the trees and the wheat fields to make them grow without effort. Thanks to her, the island's nature produced grapes and grain by itself, without the need to sow or plow.

I did my part, too. My long friendship with Aristaeus, the god of beekeeping, had taught me how to talk with bees early in my life, and I used that gift to invite dozens of their queens to build their hives on Avalon, so we could have honey worthy of gods.

We made the island in our image, to remind us of what we had lost but also of what we could save. In time, my sisters and I grew bold enough to seek the company of mortals, whom we had for generations inspired to achieve great deeds.

Poets, writers and bards lived on Albion, too, and we invited them to Avalon through dreams and visions, giving them instructions on how to undertake the sea voyage in safety. Many came; not only artists, but also people gifted in many crafts, such as smithery, jewel-setting, sculpting and pottery. We saved them from the poverty of the mainland, from the sickness, from the hunger and the war. On Avalon, they had time to develop their crafts and lived long, joyful lives.

The island of apples became a utopia of unparalleled beauty, our own Olympus in this new land.

3

THE ENCHANTRESS OF TWO
WORLDS

Time passed. A generation rolled on, replacing the previous one. My sisters and I continued to rescue artists and craftspeople from the mainland. However, a silent restlessness started growing inside me. I felt something was missing. As I walked on the shores of Avalon, my bare feet stepping on the golden sand, lined with trees heavy with fruit, I saw well-fed, content people with not a worry in the world.

But what of the people who were stuck on the mainland, who had no means to reach Avalon? What of the mothers who had to bury their children claimed by the constant state of war infesting the land? What of the hard-working shepherds and farmers who succumbed to the injustice of raiders, cutthroats and thieves, claiming the labor of their hands with a swing of a sword?

The more Avalon prospered, the more I could see the gap with Albion.

I was reminded of the words my mother had said. She had put her trust in me, had told me to act like the herald of our culture, to inspire justice and stability, and instead, I was listening to musicians entertaining me and my sisters in the safety of our halls.

No more.

I gathered my sisters and told them about Mnemosyne's last wish. They were hesitant; did not understand what I wanted. So I told them. My plan was to inspire men, through visions and dreams, who had the power to change things on the mainland. If we had learned one thing since arriving in this northern land, it was that the makers of destiny here were warriors holding swords, axes, and spears. If we spoke to them, convinced them of what was right to bring peace and prosperity, if we reached their hearts through their minds, everything would change.

"This won't work, sister," Clio said. "You can't speak of silk to a man who has seen nothing but rough wool and expect him to understand."

"We owe it to our mother," I said to her. "We ought to try."

And so we did. We inhabited the dreams of the warriors, the generals, and the conquerors, hoping to find someone worthy among them, someone with an open mind and a true heart who could lead Albion to peace and stability.

I can see now my blindness. Clio was right. I always underestimated the cultural gap between us.

These people, like their gods, followed values we did not understand, and because we didn't understand their minds, they didn't know what we were saying. As a result, our wish to give them prosperity got lost in translation.

"Maybe they don't even want the prosperity we are offering," my sister Melpomene said. "Maybe they are content with constantly being at war with each other."

"They are savages, Calliope," my sister Thalia chimed in. "They drink and bathe in blood. What did you expect? That they'd turn their heads to you, like dogs eager to please? Don't you see? If you toss gems to pigs, they'll just choke trying to swallow them."

That made all my sisters laugh.

"This is not one of your beloved comedies, Thalia," I said to her. "People are dying by the thousands just a few leagues from here. War has taken everything from them."

"War, my beloved sister, is their favorite sport," Thalia said, twirling her ebony hair. "And if you still haven't noticed that, you're twice the fool I believed you were. Come, sisters," she gestured to the others. "Let us do something fun with our time."

"Thalia," I called her.

She stopped.

"I told you of our mother's wish. What would you have me do?"

Thalia tossed a glance over my shoulder, looking briefly at the mist covering Albion; then her iron-gray eyes turned back to me. "Let them play," she said.

Her laugh echoed in the hallway until stark silence was the only company I had left.

My sisters did not help me after that day. They went back to their arts and music, shifting their focus to the wealth of Avalon and the well-being of the inhabitants.

But I couldn't, not after what Mother had said, not after knowing so much more could be done for that divided country trapped in a dark age.

I felt that I had failed the mission my mother had entrusted to me. I could not give up.

In desperation, I widened my reach and touched minds farther than ever before. I didn't limit my dreams and visions to the warriors and the conquerors; I started touching the dreams of people who had a special light that set them apart from the rest. Druids, witches, sorcerers, necromancers, and wizards. I spoke to them in images and smells, and in doing so I spread my message, with the hope some of them would understand.

For a long time, I exhausted myself in the effort while my sisters played flutes and gorged on apples and honey.

Still, I had no answer.

I could not sleep. I could not eat. Every day, I was reminded of my mother's words: "May your justice bathe the barbarian lands you shall call home and bring stability and culture along the way." I walked in silence down the long, marble hallway of our palace, looking for a solution as my frustration became desperation.

Then, one day, a boat arrived in Avalon. I received the news from one of the dock masters, who told me the only passenger aboard had requested an audience with me.

"It's a woman, my Queen," the dockmaster said. "Very beautiful and very impatient to meet you. She asked to speak with you alone."

"Bring her to me."

I was sitting on a high-backed chair when the doors of my hall were opened. A woman strode forward.

She was tall and slender, dressed in a long tunic the color of fog. Her hair was long and auburn, and it fell in waves past her shoulders.

"I rejoice in your shining presence, Calliope, Muse of eloquence and epic poetry," she said, speaking fluent High Hellenic, the language of my kin. "My name is Morgana. I dreamt your message, mighty Muse of Avalon. I come as you called, to serve as you please."

"Welcome to my house, Morgana," I said, leaning on my throne. "It is a rarity to hear my tongue spoken so fluently on foreign soil."

Morgana knelt before me, her eyes cast down. "I have travelled extensively to Greece, my lady, lived there for long years and learned many things from the great gods of the south."

"Rise," I said. "What is the art you serve, Morgana?"

The woman stood up smoothly. "I am an enchantress, my lady. I use sorcery to shape things and to bless people, to protect valuable objects with spells, and hide them for safekeeping."

Her tunic changed color, from gray to pearl white, matching the marble of the floor.

I frowned. "You speak of magic."

"Isn't it a form of art in its own right, mightiest of the Muses?" Morgana waved a hand, and a climbing plant the color of red windflowers appeared around one of the nearby columns. "Magic is the way my kind shapes nature into a better version of itself. Enchanters change the face of things; make them stronger or more resilient. We can also hide things from view, or present them in a different light."

"You will forgive me, Morgana, but I am not familiar with this kind of magic."

"Do you know the goddess Circe, my lady?" she asked.

I blinked at hearing the name. "The witch of Aiaia, daughter of Helios? I've heard of her, yes."

"My powers are like hers, and Medea's. Also like the god Hermes, and other deities keen in witchcraft."

"You speak of my people as if you knew them."

"I have been a disciple of the great goddess Hecate, who taught me witchcraft, gave me knowledge of herbs, magic mushrooms, and poisonous plants. I spoke to many demigods and a few gods before the Great Downfall of Olympus. I left there when the ashes were still warm."

I felt my heartbeat quickening. Maybe she knew something I did not. "Have you news from my home? Have some gods survived?"

Shadows bathed Morgana's face. She waved her hand again, and the red plant disappeared from the column. "Only ashes remain, my lady. The few gods who survived are scattered and hiding, as their temples were reduced to dust."

For a long time I remained quiet, the weight of Morgana's words crushing my heart. I had remained on Avalon for so long I had almost forgotten about my homeland. Maybe I could have gone back and helped. I put a hand over my chest, and I exhaled.

Morgana must have seen my pain. "There was nothing you could have done," she said, shaking her head. "But you still have the power to change things here. I've listened to your dilemma, and I came to aid you."

I shifted on my chair. "You think you can help?"

"In my presumption, I do."

"Speak then, Morgana. What do you suggest? What would you do to solve my predicament?"

"Your godly gift enables you to speak the many languages of this land, but this power can be misleading. Knowing a language doesn't mean understanding the culture that harbors it. The people of this land are a world apart from yours. They are not persuaded the way you think people should be, and what is a good deed for you might be an act of weakness for them."

"What do these people follow, then?"

"They follow power and bravery, endurance and strength. Believe me, I know it for a fact. They are my people. Men in this land are not inspired by works of art but by great deeds accomplished by carrying a sword."

"Tell me, Morgana. Why do you want to help?"

"Because I believe your heart is pure and that you care about my people. I look at what you did here in Avalon with wonder and respect and wish you could replicate it in Britain. You could save countless people by spreading this peace. I want to be a part of it."

I looked into Morgana's eyes, and for the first time in years, I saw hope. She might have answers I had always needed; she could be the bridge between my culture and the culture of the people living in Albion.

I opened my arms, and I made her my honored guest. "Sit beside me, Morgana, and tell me more about the men and the gods of this land."

And that is how Morgana came to be my counselor.

4

A ZEUS AMONG MORTALS

For weeks, Morgana stood by my side, sharing her knowledge and answering my questions.

She convinced me that the only way to understand a culture is to live like a part of it. She suggested sleeping in the woods at night, with just a mantle as a blanket and a folded rag as a pillow, to feel the insecurity of not having a roof above my head, to taste the kind of thoughts the cold wind brings in your dreams. She encouraged me to eat northern food that had never touched my mouth: dried cod, salted herring, and many varieties of smoked fish. Soups and stews made thick by almonds were put in front of me, along with hard cheese with a powerful smell and many kinds of odd-shaped beans and cereals.

My sisters did not understand. They did not understand why I spent time on a cause worth nothing, bringing with me a woman who smelled like musk and talked with beasts.

The barbarians can't be saved, they insisted, and so all they did was spend their time sighing over what we'd lost, instead of working on what might be gained by enlightening the people of Albion.

I ignored them, their judging eyes and their mocking smiles, as I walked on the island dressed in little more than rags to feel my skin exposed to the elements. I was on a mission, and I knew

Morgana had given me the much sought-after answers I needed to create a plan.

"*Britain*," Morgana corrected me one day, "Not Albion, my lady. Few would know what you mean by that name."

"Britain," I repeated the word, tasting its exotic flavor. "Tell me more about the Britons, the Welsh, and Inis Ealga. Tell me about the Picts and the Scots and the local chieftains and the secluded monks. Tell me everything you know."

Morgana did. I spent more time with her than with all my sisters.

A few weeks after she arrived on Avalon, Morgana came to me with a gift, something wrapped in long leaves, bound by a golden string.

"What is it?" I asked.

"Open it."

Inside, I found what appeared to be a dress of a sort. I took it out of its wrappings. It was light but sturdy. It seemed to be made of shells and smelled like pines and salt and river water. It was green, woven with golden threads. It took me a while to understand it wasn't a dress.

"Armor?" I said, blinking.

"A garment worthy of the Muse of Avalon," Morgana said, bowing. "I had a druid make it for you. It has magic in it. It shall keep you cool under the sun and warm when it's too cold. A warrior wears protective garments because a fight is never far, and death is waiting around every corner. Most men eat with it, sleep with it, wear it like a second skin. Your people walked in sandals, with a light dress made of silk and much of the body exposed. Britain is no such land. By wearing this, you wear a part of our culture."

The light armor fit me nicely. It came with a headdress that, too, was green and golden. When I looked at myself in the mirror, I did not look like a frail Muse anymore. I looked proud and fierce.

"How does it feel?"

"It feels strange."

"Good," Morgana said. "Very good."

I wore the armor in place of my silk dress. I wore it when walking and when sleeping. I tried to carry myself as the people of

Britain did. My mind needed to be open to anything that could help me understand the ways of the northerners.

Then came the day when Morgana and I discussed the gods my sisters and I met on our first visit to Albion.

"I'm not surprised they hunted you," Morgana said. "Our gods are bloody and territorial. They have no genuine leader and follow no order. There is nothing like Olympus here, or a great, powerful god like Zeus ruling over everything. There is only a void that invites anarchy. The world of the mortals is a projection of this chaos. What you call Albion is not a country, just a collection of tribes and clans who would destroy each other. Their only thoughts are fixed on today, on keeping their stomachs full and avoiding the blade that is chasing them, for one more day."

I thought about what she said. "You cannot build stability and prosperity on an empty stomach," I agreed.

"No, my lady. You cannot."

"How would you build a stable country, then? One that would ensure them the safety they seek?"

Morgana looked lost for a moment, then she said, "I would give them a leader."

"A leader," I repeated, "like a Zeus among the mortals."

Morgana smiled. "I was jesting, my lady. There is no such man here."

"Yet," I said.

Morgana folded her arms. "I admire your spirit. I truly believe your intent is honorable, and yet ..." she trailed off, her eyes wandering, as though chasing the ghost of a thought but never grasping it.

"Say it," I gestured for her to continue. "What do you believe? That I am chasing a fantasy? A delusion?"

"A very bold plan," she said with a pacifying gesture. "You have done much here in Avalon. Maybe, mighty Muse, you can be content with what you and your sisters achieved."

"I cannot stand and watch the innocent die while we bathe in clean water and bask in the sun," I told her. "Yes, there is selfishness and barbarism across the water, but there is value and courage, too. These people need a leader capable of bringing them together. We just need to find such a man."

Morgana paused. She brushed her hands together and said nothing.

"You're thinking something," I said. "What is it? Speak your mind."

"There might be a way," she said slowly. "But it will be risky."

"Tell me the way."

"We could give them a symbol of power," she said. "Something basic. Something that anyone would understand and respect. People would gather around one such symbol."

"A symbol of power," I repeated. I thought of everything I had learned from Morgana about the tribes and the chieftain clans, and about the history woven in battles and acts of bravery. Every single man respected, more than feared, death. It was like a lover they might lie with at the end of each day. I stood silent and pondered that for a little. What is it that brings death, I asked myself. Many things, but what is it that these people control and do not fear? What is it that they respect? A rite? A story? A tool? Then an idea surfaced.

"A weapon," I said, thinking aloud.

"My lady?"

I turned toward my counselor. "What about a sword?" I said.

"A sword," Morgana mused. "Yes, that is something anyone would understand. It symbolizes power and control, but also sovereignty and justice."

"Then it is decided," I said, rising. "We shall give them the mightiest sword mankind has ever seen."

5

THE SWORD IN THE STONE

I summoned the best blacksmith on Avalon and made him forge the sword. For three days and three nights, the blacksmith worked without pause. I blessed him with stamina no mortal could have possessed, and I guided his hands as I had guided Homer's and Virgil's and those of countless other artists throughout history. The blacksmith had forged many swords for kings and princes in his long years, but what he presented me with on the third night was unlike anything he had ever made.

"Here, my Queen," he said, kneeling in front of me. "I give you the best work my hands have ever forged."

And it was. As the minds of the writers and the poets I had inspired had created the best works in the history of mankind, so this blacksmith had crafted the best sword a mortal could forge.

"It's beautiful," Morgana said, looking at the weapon with eyes wide open. "This is indeed a sword of legend."

I took the sword in my hand, looked at the blue-gray metal, and saw myself reflected on the blade; my long chestnut braid, my pale skin, my green eyes and my full lips. The ease I had when I lived in Greece was gone from my eyes. I still looked young, but there were deep lines on my forehead that spoke of lost things. I looked at my counselor. "Now," I said, "the sword needs a scabbard of equal value."

The scabbard I made myself. When it was done, I asked Morgana to put her magic in it.

"The scabbard will have the true value," I said to her. "He who wields this scabbard shall not lose a single drop of blood. As long as a mortal wears it, it will prevent death from any wound caused by a weapon."

"Why the scabbard, my lady?" she asked, puzzled. "Why not the sword?"

"Anyone would think the sword must hold the true power. In reality, the value is in the things we least expect. Trust me; this will help weed out the worthy from the unworthy." I held both the scabbard and the sword in my hands, but I didn't explain myself further, even though I saw curiosity in Morgana's eyes.

"These are magnificent works of craftsmanship, my lady. A true achievement."

"Look closely, Morgana. These are just tools necessary to our goal. Now we need the man."

Morgana bowed before me. "Yes, my lady."

"You are hesitant," I sensed. "What is wrong?"

"Now comes the risky part," she said. "Are you still confident in your plan?"

"We already discussed this. We both agreed it was necessary. To choose a worthy man, we need a worthy way of judging him. I am the only way."

"Yes." She diverted her eyes from me. "I can turn you into the soul of the sword, mighty Calliope. But once I've cast my spell upon you, you might have to wait a long time for the worthy man you're seeking."

"I will take the risk. People are dying as we speak, Morgana. I will have no further discussion."

"As you command." She looked at the weapon. "A sword needs a name, my lady. It carries better its legend. What shall you call it?"

The sword was glinting at me, its hilt cool to the touch. "Let the people of this land decide the name of their own legend."

"A wise choice."

"You have already found a location for the sword-seekers, haven't you?"

Morgana nodded. "It's a mountain in the middle of a harsh land where nothing but scorpions and poisonous snakes survive."

"Cast your spells on that mountain," I ordered. "Make the climb itself worthy of a song. I will take care of spreading the story of the sword in the stone. By the time I'm done, we will have people by the hundreds eager to draw it."

On the next day, I summoned men to travel throughout Britain and to the lands in the north to spread the story of the sword in the stone. He who drew the sword from the rock would become the king of a nation. He would have to prove his valor by reaching its top, then his acumen by solving a riddle, and then his spirit of sacrifice by finally drawing the weapon out of the mountaintop.

What I was looking for was a man with the heart of a poet and the mind of a leader. Only such a man could succeed, the very example of what they valued in this land: valor, sharp wit, and courage.

Fewer than half the messengers I sent came back to Avalon. They were ragged and wounded, and shadows besieged their eyes.

"What happened to the rest of the men?" I asked the leader.

"We spread the word, my Queen, as you ordered," the messenger said. "But the mainland is in chaos. Countless warriors are coming from the continent, some say from Germania. They speak a foreign tongue and wave great battle axes. They are raiding Britain as we speak and bringing havoc."

"Warriors from Germania, you say? What are they called?"

"They call them Saxon, my Queen."

I looked at Morgana, sitting on a chair beside me. Thoughts glazed her eyes.

"They are dangerous, bloodthirsty warriors, Calliope," she said. "Strong and proud. If they mean to invade Britain, I'm afraid there won't be much left when they are done."

I turned to the messenger. "How many?"

"Enough to cover the entire country with blood, my Queen."

"We need to speed our effort," I said to Morgana. "Now, more than ever, Britain needs its hero."

We left Avalon at once, without ceremony, without even telling my sisters.

Morgana brought me to the top of the mountain she had chosen.

"The first man is just now climbing the mountain, my lady," she said, looking down.

"Good," I said. I looked at the sword. It had already been thrust inside the mountaintop, along with the scabbard. "It is time. Do it."

She bowed her head low and spread her arms. "As you command."

I felt a chilly wind brush past me, then my feet were lifted, and I lost all sense of time. I closed my eyes, and when I opened them again, I was looking at the world through the sword. I *was* the sword.

Something wasn't right. I asked Morgana to make me able to come and go from the sword as I pleased, but I found myself trapped in it.

"In truth," Morgana said, flicking her long hair, "I can't believe you fell for it. You really are a fool, as your sisters said." A smile full of mirth made her look like a different person. "There is no such man as the one you seek in this land, or on any land, my lady. You made my life so easy. Now that you are out of the way, I can make your throne my own."

Her arms moved like snakes, and her appearance changed. Her loosened hair became a braid, her skin turned pale, and the color of her eyes became emerald green.

"How do I look?" She mocked me with my own voice. "Your sisters will never notice the difference. I have learned everything about you in these months. But don't despair. You have been kind to me, and I'll share the same kindness with you. I made sure your stay here is comfortable. I have kept your senses alive. Smell, sight, hearing, and touch; you'll be able to see and feel the world around you. Only, you won't be able to talk or to leave the sword. But if a man comes with the qualities you seek and releases you from the stone, you shall be free. See, I can be fair."

"Why, Morgana?" I said, knowing she could listen with her mind.

"Why?" she repeated. "Still you don't understand. This is not Greece, Calliope. We take what we want in this land. We walk on the heads of weaklings like you. There is no place for your kind here. You deserve that stone."

"What about the Saxons?" I said. "What about the slaughtering of thousands of people? Don't you have a conscience for the women and the children who will perish?"

"Haven't you learned, Calliope? For men, there is no finer art than war, and I am its Muse."

Morgana disappeared in a flicker of light.

I tried hard to leave the sword, to use my powers to undo whatever thing Morgana did to me. Nothing changed.

Not a day has passed that I don't regret my stupidity.

I have been on this mountaintop for what feels like an eternity. What at the beginning had been a quest filled with hope has in time become a shard of presumption that is decaying in my heart, a hopeless effort that is gathering dust.

Morgana was right. There are no such men as I hoped for. There is only greed and lust for power.

It hurts me to admit this, but I believe this land is without hope and destined for doom.

6

THE NIGHT SEEKER

A long time has passed since Morgana's deceit, and every day I am reminded of my failure. I know that without the stability I wished for, people are suffering. The Saxons have in all likelihood continued the bloodbath. Not only was I unable to share my culture and to bring stability, I welcomed a snake to my bosom and trusted her with my life.

There is nothing I can do now, except hope against hope that there really is a man with the qualities I seek to unite this land and fight the invaders.

It has the probability of a coin landing on its edge, but still, it is better than nothing.

The moon is a silver sickle set in the night sky. The air is crisp and quiet. I wonder what my sisters are doing. Are they well? Has Morgana's treachery harmed them? Questions upon questions storm my mind and fill my heart with dread.

I hear the low buzz before I see the bee approaching from the patch of bushes on the edge of the mountaintop, and I shift my attention to the insect.

"Hello, my dear," I greet her as she rests on my hilt. "What news do you bring?"

Bees are the only company I have. They are the only living creatures I know how to talk to. They have made my long isolation somehow more manageable.

The bee's yellow body vibrates.

"A small group of men, you say," I vibrate back to her, "camping not far away from here. Well, that would not be surprising. Probably mercenaries coming to try their luck, tomorrow. We've had our fair share in the last few weeks, haven't we? Oh, there is something else?" I wait for her to stop moving. "Are you sure? A man is climbing, you say? Right now?"

The insect vibrates her assent, her small wings flickering pearl white in the moonlight.

"It cannot be," I say to her. "Only a madman would climb the mountain in this darkness."

Again the insect moves her body.

"That is true," I say. "All the scorpions and the snakes sleep at night, there's that. But still, it's easier to misplace a foot in the darkness. I wonder what would push a man to try his luck like that."

I listen to the air, waiting for the thud of a body falling, crashing against the distant bottom, but I hear nothing but the sound of the wind brushing the dry plants.

One hour passes, then two. Finally, I glimpse a movement on the edge of the mountaintop, then a hand roughly grasping the cliff, and then a head emerges. A body lifts itself up and then rolls on its side. The newcomer is breathing heavily, his back on the ground and his chest rising and falling.

I can see the climbing must have cost him much of his strength. He stays down for a long time, then he finally rises. It's difficult to see his features in the darkness. All I can see in the moonlight is that he looks short and frail.

The man looks around quickly. He barely glances at me, as if just to make sure I'm here, that this is the right mountain, then he takes something from his travel bag and eats it. He kindles no fire and uses a blanket to shield himself from the cold. A soft tune rises, breaking the silence. The stranger's voice is soft, woven with a peculiar sort of melancholy. I can't catch the words, but I like their musicality.

The tune stops when the night seeker lies down and sleeps.

My curiosity only increases. If Helios were here, I would bribe him to take on his chariot faster to shorten Selene's reign. Then I remember that probably both of them are dead and the little good mood I had disappears.

I will have to wait out the night for answers.

7

THE PRICE OF JUSTICE IS
ALWAYS RED

The seeker sleeps until the first light of the sun kindles the horizon before exploding into a blazing crown of orange and gold.

There are a few clouds in the sky, but not enough to summon rain. The wind is thick with the smell of smoke.

As the first light of the day bathes the mountaintop, the seeker stirs, then he rises, and I can finally give him a first good look.

He appears little more than a boy, probably the youngest seeker who has reached the mountaintop. I've never been good with mortal ages, but my guess is that he might be fifteen, maybe sixteen years old. His skin is fair, and his hair is the same gold of the first light of the day.

The young man stretches, then relieves himself on the edge of the mountain. When he's done, he rummages inside his travel sack and takes out some food. The morning wind suggests he's breaking his fast with flatbread, smoked cod, and hard cheese.

Again he hums a song, and this time I catch some words. I'm surprised to find it's Latin he's singing. My curiosity only increases. Rome fell long ago, and this seeker doesn't have the olive skin and the dark eyes of the heirs of the eagle's empire. He might be a nobleman of mixed Roman-Briton origins, but still, his look speaks of northern origins. I study his clothes. He wears a wool jacket and heavy boots. On his belt there is a long knife and two small leather sacks. A red dragon is sewn on his mantle. The symbol draws my eyes more than anything. There is a message there to decipher, but I have not enough information to do much more than weave hypotheses.

What is certain is that the young man barely regards me for the entire time. Instead, he takes great care in inspecting the surrounding area. He looks at the scabbard, then he walks in front of the words I made Morgana engrave into the rock:

Draw me, friend, by paying your due in worth instead of strength, for the price of justice is always red.

He reads the riddle, then rereads again. Only when his lips have tasted the sentence a dozen times does he finally look at me.

His green eyes are lively and looking at every inch of my exposed surface, as if trying to unveil a great secret.

"Hail, mighty sword in the stone," he says, his voice carrying the same musicality he had while he was singing. "I've heard a lot about you. I must admit I am not disappointed. You look as beautiful as the legend suggests."

He walks toward me, and as I think his hands will close around my hilt, I'm almost disappointed to see him stop a few steps away. He picks up a small stone as flat as a coin from the ground, then sits, legs crossed, his eyes always on me. "Tove the Unholy tried for two days and two nights to get you out of this mountaintop and failed." He weighs the stone in his hand, then tosses it and catches it without looking. "He is twice my size and has three times my strength. That says to me that I should probably save my breath and labor with my brain." His eyes wander over the cliff. Then he looks over the horizon, where a river is sneaking its way through another mountain. The clouds shift toward the east, and for some time, the young man watches them moving. Then his eyes come back to me.

"But then what of Cameron, the cunning Gaelic thief? He also tried to draw you and failed. I've heard stories about him. He could have stolen an egg yolk without cracking the shell."

He stands and starts walking around me like a lion circling his prey. "But no matter what you made us believe all this time, you are no puzzle, sword in the stone. No. You are a Gordian knot."

The young man rolls the small stone on his knuckles and uses his thumb to push it across the back of his finger. Then, he raises his middle finger and uses it to push one side of the stone down so that the stone moves onto the back of his middle finger. He keeps performing that trick smoothly as he looks at me.

"Longevo the Wise, Dughall Strongborn, Godwin of the Storm-light, Asmund Heart of Ice." He pronounces each name with reverence, as would have done a bard naming heroes from a great song. "The list goes on and on. You bested some of the strongest and brightest glory-seekers the world has to offer. It really looks like you don't want to get drawn from that stone, do you?"

Of course I want to be drawn, you insolent brat, I snap, even though I know he can't hear me. *Drawing me out of here is the whole point!*

But something else surfaces. Did I make the trial too difficult? Perhaps I reached too far, based my plan on nothing more than wishful thinking. What if this boy is making plain what has been clear to everyone else but me?

A fool, Morgana called me. Maybe she was right.

"You want valor and strength," the young seeker continues. "You want wisdom. But you also want sacrifice, don't you?"

He glances at the riddle; then he covers the distance that separates us.

"There is only one sacrifice that could prove with no doubt the commitment of a man to the cause of justice, who believes the needs of the many outweigh the needs of the few. And that commitment cannot be found from a man who thinks he will climb down from this mountain."

He let the flat stone fall from his fingers. His expression is grim now. He looks at his hands; the muscles on his arms are tense. "Yes," he nods as if reading something written on his palm. "The price of justice is always red."

He places his right wrist on the sharp edge of the sword and presses hard against it. His veins open, blood pours down like a river. The metal of the sword is dull with his blood.

He breathes through clenched teeth; pain flashes in his eyes, but he keeps them on me. With his left hand he grabs my hilt and pulls.

A sharp sound ripples against the stone, like a spear clashing against marble. I feel the bottom part of the sword reflecting sunlight after who knows how long.

The seeker holds me up, and I shine like a daylight star. I feel something grasping at my chest and yanking me out of the sword. When I open my eyes again, I am back in my divine body, crouched on the rough ground of the mountaintop.

The young man looks at me. "Who are you?" Then his eyes widen, and he falls on his knees. "Virgin Mary?" For a second, he seems to forget about the mortal wound on his wrist. "Have you come to aid me? Or am I dead already?"

"I'm no virgin," I say to him, rising. "And my name is Calliope."

"Calliope?"

"Yes. I was trapped inside the sword."

"What? How could you ..." He groans, never finishes the sentence. He drops to the ground like a sack of stones, his arm now crimson red.

"Wear the scabbard!" I urge him, knowing that Morgana's magic prevents me from helping him. "It will keep you from bleeding to death."

He glances at the sword's case. "What? That ... that scabbard?"

"Do you see any other? Yes, that one! Take it."

He rises and trudges toward the scabbard. Now that he has broken the spell, he pulls it out with ease. As soon as he dons it, the bleeding stops and the wound closes.

"Magic," he breathes out. He looks at me. "How is it possible?"

"Sit," I tell him. "You can't die from weapon wounds, but you could fall from lack of strength and break your neck. Sit, I said."

"I'm fine," he mumbles. "I just—"

"Sit."

His body sways dangerously. "Yes," he says, bobbing his head. "That might be wise."

"Here, let me help you." I help him down.

The seeker sighs, then looks at me, blinking. "Are you ... are you a hallucination?"

"Quiet, boy. We need to get your strength back." I look around in search of his travel sack. I find it and bring it to him.

"What are you—"

"I said, *quiet*. I'm thinking." I look inside the travel sack, but I find nothing useful except for water. I try to remember something Asclepius, the Greek god of medical arts, told me once; something about wounded humans. He said that after bleeding, mortals need to replenish their blood to survive. Eating and drinking is an excellent way of doing it, but some foods are better than others.

The young man looks at me, wondering. "What are you thinking?" he asks.

"Something a friend once said."

"A friend?"

"Yes." I look at him. "Do you have beef or liver?"

He shakes his head.

"What about poultry? What about cheese? Do you have some?"

"Cheese? Yes." He searches in one of the small sacks latched on his belt. "I have some here."

"Eat it. Then drink. It will take a while to build up your strength, but this will speed up the process."

I watch him eating and drinking. Unfortunately, his face is pale and getting paler. I take out a few strings of dried fish he has left from the night before and let him eat those, too.

"I feel the world spinning," the young man says.

"I think that's normal."

"Is it? Why am I even listening to you? You still haven't proven you're not a hallucination."

I smile, then pinch his shoulder.

"Ouch!"

"Does that give you an answer?"

A few minutes pass. I see his eyelids getting heavier. "Calliope, you said you're called," he pauses, then smirks, as if realizing something funny. "Do you know you have the same name as the Muse of poetry?"

"Yes," I say, brushing his hair back. "Yes, I know. Now rest. You did very well, young man. Rest. There will be time to talk later." I kiss him on the forehead and give him the blessing of Morpheus.

8

THE KINGSLAYER

I keep the boy's head on my lap. He sleeps through the entire morning.

Never had I thought a seeker so young would draw the sword. I'm thankful but surprised. I was expecting a seasoned man with a lifetime of experience to achieve the goal. Destiny has a peculiar sense of humor.

I put a hand on the boy's forehead, to make sure his mind isn't wandering in ominous places. I am relieved to find he has no fever.

When he opens his eyes again, he smiles at me. "You're still here," he says.

"You sound surprised."

"A beautiful woman appeared out of nowhere after I drew a magical sword from a stone. Yes, I'm surprised."

"A hero and an adulator. How do you feel?"

"Better." He looks at his wrist, then at the scabbard he is wearing. "So it really happened."

"This scabbard is magic," I explain. "As long as you wear it, it will prevent death from any wound caused by a weapon."

"Where is the sword?"

"It's right beside you."

He fumbles around with his hands until he feels the metal of the weapon. He puts the sword in the scabbard, and only then he calms down. "Good. I can't lose you."

"Tell me," I ask him. "Do you often talk with inanimate objects?"

He flashes his teeth at me in a child-like smile. "Do plants count?"

"You're trying to be funny."

"Am I succeeding?"

"Barely."

The young man rises and stretches.

"What brought you here?" I ask him.

His expression becomes serious. "A promise I made to my uncle."

"Well, young seeker, rejoice. The promise you made, you kept."

"Now you tell me something, Calliope. Why were you inside the sword?"

I see no harm in telling him my story, so I talk. The sun has climbed down half of the sky when I'm done talking.

The boy looks at me for a long time. "You are saying you really are the Muse Calliope?"

"That is so."

"I preferred to think of you as a hallucination. It made things easier."

"Things seldom are."

"But why are you here? I mean, in Britain."

"That's another story, and I'm sure you're eager to join your friends camped at the foot of the mountain. They must be worried about you."

He looks at me as if I made a jest. "What friends?" he asks. "What camp? I came alone."

"Men are camped close to here." I point over the cliff. "I thought you came with them."

He walks near the cliff and looks to where I'm pointing. His eyes widen.

I frown. "What's wrong?"

He has no time to explain.

We hear the grunt coming from our right and turn to look. A huge man is heaving himself up and over the mountaintop, with a hand as big as my torso.

The young seeker steps back. His hand flashes on the hilt of the sword. The muscles on his neck are tense, his eyes filled with horror.

"Ah!" the giant bellows. He stands up and pats his hands on his legs to remove the dust. "That was a climb to make with both eyes open!" His eyes find us. "What is this? A boy and a girl?" The man's accent is thick. The words roll strangely between sentences. "Mighty Woden! Am I on the wrong mountain?" His eyes catch the sword in the boy's hand. "Oho." His smile is broad and crooked. "There it is!"

The boy draws the sword from the scabbard. "Drefan the kingslayer," he says. His voice betrays no emotion, but his eyes speak of hate and fear.

"In the flesh!" the giant roars. "Do I know you, boy?"

"Your brother slaughtered King Vortigern at a peace council," the young seeker says, speaking the words like a poisonous spell. "He and his men drew their knives on sacred soil and killed hundreds of Britons' chiefs."

"Gyse." The giant bobs his head, his smile wide. "You're talking of the Night of the Long Knives. I was there when it happened. And how do you know who I am?"

"You killed my uncle on the battlefield while he was defending Britain from you and your demon men."

"Did I?" He spreads his arms. "What was your uncle's name?"

"Ambrosius Aurelianus."

He taps his head with an index finger. "The name means nothing to me. You Britons all look and sound the same."

"I already claimed the sword in the stone," the seeker says, showing it to Drefan. "It's mine."

"Gyse," Drefan assents. "Well, I guess now I will have to claim it from the stiff fingers of your corpse. It won't be much of a song they'll sing, but we all make do with what we have."

He takes a huge battle-axe from his back and points it at the boy.

"Stop, Saxon!" I put myself between the two warriors. "You cannot claim what this seeker has already gained. Whoever draws the sword first is the true King of Britain."

The giant looks at me as if I were made of glass. "Why, I don't want to be king of this land of pigs, you wench. I just want the sword."

The boy flexes his legs, readying himself for the battle. "You'll have to get it first."

The Saxon smiles. "It shall be a great pleasure."

I look at the boy. "Wait! You can't—"

But he has already moved against Drefan.

It is in moments like these I wish I were a mighty goddess able to move mountains and break an anvil with a touch. But I'm a different kind of goddess, one whose power resides in her words, and all I can do is stand to the side and watch the duel unfolding.

The boy is fast and can move on his feet like a dancer, but I can clearly see where the fight is heading. Drefan is a more seasoned warrior, his movement more careful and experienced, and he duels like the whole confrontation is nothing but an exercise to entertain him. It's only a question of time before he has the upper hand.

"That's the problem with you Britons," Drefan says as he easily avoids one of the boy's blows. "You fight like women, moving your feet as if cleaning them of dirt. Own your blows, boy. Just like this."

He punches the boy's stomach, and the young seeker falls to the ground.

Drefan laughs. "Take your time," he says. "Have some water while you are at it. I'm having fun with you. You're a good sport."

"You talk too much," the young seeker says.

"Are you well?" I ask. I start walking toward him, but he points the sword at me.

"Stay!" he says. "I hold the sword in the stone. Nothing can stop me."

"Who is she?" the giant teases. "Your sister? No? Your lover? I bet she's a better fighter than you are."

The boy stands, and the battle dance resumes.

"Good!" Drefan cheers, swinging his axe and deflecting his opponent's blow with ease. "The last one, I almost felt. Harder now. The blades are barely kissing, Briton. Come on. Put your heart in it."

The boy loses his balance, and the Saxon thrusts a knee in his stomach.

"Ah!" Drefan roars, "I think I broke something, didn't I? Well, it was fun while it lasted, I'll give you that. Now, young man, I will knock the brains out of your head."

He is about to swing his axe when I throw a stone at his head, and catch his eye.

Drefan screams. "You whore!" He holds the side of his head, blood in his hand. "I'll fuck your corpse when I'm done with him!"

That gives the boy enough time to stand and pick up the sword.

"Are you okay, my lady?" he says.

"Don't think of me. Watch out!"

Too late. The Saxon's hand closes around the boy's arm and forces him to drop the sword on the ground. The giant grabs the young seeker by the neck, turns him around and brings him up against his chest.

"Time to say goodbye," he growls while putting an arm around the boy's neck. "But first, tell me your name. You're little more than a child, but you fought with valor. I might bury you with honor somewhere in this cursed land."

I watch the boy slowly taking his long knife from his belt. The Saxon's eye is bleeding, and he doesn't notice his movement.

The boy says something.

"What did you say?" Drefan asks, coming closer.

"I said, my name is Arthur Pendragon." His hand jerks to the side and he thrusts his long knife inside his own belly, so that the blade cuts through him and the Saxon both.

Drefan roars in pain. He releases Arthur, his hands trying to stop the blood pouring out of his stomach. His mouth is stained with red; there is surprise on his face. "You ... crazy Briton," he says. He spits on the ground. "What ... what were you thinking?"

"I don't think much," Arthur says, staggering. His wound has already started healing. He pushes Drefan over the cliff, the Saxon's stupefied smile still stamped on his face.

I watch Drefan fall like a doll down the mountain.

Arthur drops to the ground, breathing heavily.

"Did I kill him?" he asks me.

"Yes. You killed him."

"Good," he says. Then he glances over the cliff to the horizon. "Only a few thousand left."

I smile at him. "You won't have to fight them all. Not yet, and not alone. With that sword, the Britons will gather around you, and you will lead them to victory."

"Why does everything you say sound so good, my lady?"

"I think you have lost too much blood. You're in pain, and yet you smile."

Arthur groans. "Are you going to say I need to rest?"

"Probably. I'm not sure."

"Why are you smiling, my lady?"

"Because I found my man after all."

This time, I need not send a pacifying sleep over him. He passes out.

I lean over his chest, and I am relieved to hear his heart pumping steadily.

I take his mantle off and fold it into a pillow I put underneath his head. I look up. The horizon is blood red; another day is about to end.

I hold a hand up and wait. After a few seconds, I hear the buzz and a bee rests on my palm.

"The men you warned me about," I say to her. "I want them far from here when we climb our way down. Nobody can know we are coming."

The bee flies high, and after a while, I can feel the air roaring with a buzz. This time, the swarm that appears from behind the bush is big enough to shadow the entire mountaintop. The bees are not alone. They have brought with them red-striped wasps and hornets as black as coal.

The cloud of insects flies down, and I know I won't have to worry about Saxons when we reach the bottom.

I look at Arthur and wonder what his story is. I suspect we will come to know each other better in the next days. I know destiny wanted us to meet, and I know he is the answer I was waiting for.

I look at myself. I'm still wearing the armor Morgana gave me long ago. I take it off, piece by piece, and toss it over the cliff. I see it bouncing down and down, breaking into pieces.

I am dressed in nothing more than a tunic now, but for the first time in a long time, I feel secure and in control.

I will be fine. This land will be fine. And the promise I made to my mother will become a statement of defiance that I will carry with me as a torch.

I will no longer be bound to what my past self believed to be right and wrong. Greece belongs to my past. My future lies in the midst of this land. I will listen to the world that surrounds me, and to the people living in it, starting with this young man called Arthur.

It's ironic how things change. When I first arrived in the north, I criticized the British gods for being blood-hungry, then I elected myself a sacrifice of blood as the means to deciding my champion.

Yes, things do change. I will no longer think of myself as a Greek goddess. I have become what this land made me, a seeker of men who can do good, not through words but through great deeds sanctioned by a sword.

Calliope died when my mother kissed me at the ruin of my home.

What's left of her are memories and sorrow.

I am not her anymore. I am the Muse of Avalon.

The End

~

The saga continues in 'Olympians, Demigods and Rebels'!

AUTHOR'S NOTE

This is it.

You've reached the end of this box set. I've put my heart and soul into each of these stories. I treasure every moment I spend writing them.

You are a reader. I believe savvy authors use reader's feedback to improve their craft.

There are two ways I do this. Here's the first way: I read feedback. I am a big believer in feedback. Why? The author learns something new about their craft. Future readers get better stories in return. It's a win-win.

I'd be grateful if you took a moment to send me an email to let me know what you liked about my stories, or didn't like. Your time is precious, and I thank you for it.

You can fire an email at hello@micheleamitrani.com.

The second way I learn is by reading reviews. If there was something you particularly loved about the stories I'd be grateful if you'd post a review in the online store where you bought this box set.

Review on your favorite store

Thank you.

Michele Amitrani

ACKNOWLEDGMENTS

Thank you to Alessandro, Mana, Sev, Doro, Donna, Lena, Rafael, Mark, Crystal and Victoria for reading these stories and providing valuable feedback.

You helped me share the stories I was meant to tell.

ABOUT THE AUTHOR

I am an independent author living in Rome, the Eternal City. I grew up writing of falling empires, space battles, mortal betrayals, monumental decisions, and everything in between.

I wrote and published my first English book, *Lord of Time*, in between waiting tables and occasionally exploring the world.

I now spend my days traveling through time and space and, more often than not, writing about impossible but necessary worlds.

When I'm not busy training dragons or mastering the Force, you can find me at MicheleAmitrani.com or hanging out on Face-book at /MicheleAmitraniAuthor.

A genius boy turned dreamer of the future. He has a vision to make a better tomorrow and will gain strategic allies over his life to set the stage for success. His vision - Polaris and outer space. If you love the endless possibilities and challenges of space exploration, *Rise of Polaris* is for you. >> **Get your copy now.**